MORE SPOOKY STORIES

MORE SPOOKY STORIES

TANUSHREE & AJOY PODDER

illustrated by
SUCHARITA SENGUPTA SURI

HarperCollins *Publishers* India

First published in India by HarperCollins *Publishers* in 2022
4th Floor, Tower A, Building No. 10, Phase II, DLF Cyber City,
Gurugram, Haryana – 122002
www.harpercollins.co.in

2 4 6 8 10 9 7 5 3 1

P-ISBN: 978-93-5629-479-0
E-ISBN: 978-93-5629-480-6

Typeset in 12/16 Chaparral Pro at
Manipal Technologies Limited, Manipal

Printed and bound at
Thomson Press (India) Ltd.

MIX
Paper
FSC FSC® C010615

This book is produced from independently certified FSC® paper
to ensure responsible forest management.

'For my favourite aunt, Reba Mukherjee, who was a brilliant raconteur with a marvellous sense of humour. She taught me to look at the brighter side of life.'

CONTENTS

PRELUDE

The bumpy road made Uday Sengupta cling tightly to the door as the taxi raced through the wilderness in the darkness. The mud track, pitted with gaping holes and craters, made the journey much more uncomfortable, but the driver paid no attention to Uday's requests to slow down or drive carefully.

It had been almost two hours since they had started on their way and now that the destination was just a few minutes away, the driver, keen to get back to the city at the earliest, sped as though chased by demons.

I'm going to be so glad to get there – especially in one piece, thought the young passenger, clutching the headrest of the passenger seat in front of him. 'Can't you go a *little* slower?' he snapped, gnashing his teeth.

'No, Babu, I don't want to be stuck in this godforsaken place at night – it's not safe,' replied the driver.

'You don't have to go back to the city! My uncle has a huge house, and there's lots of accommodation for the staff. I can arrange for you to spend the night there.'

'Thank you, Babu, but I prefer to sleep in my own bed,' the driver grinned insolently. They were about a kilometre from the house when the driver made a sharp U-turn.

'What are you doing?' yelled Uday. Ruffled and exhausted, he was not in a mood for tricks.

'You'll have to get off here because I'm going back. It's already dark, and the streetlights aren't working. Also, there seems to be no electricity – I don't want to be stuck here!'

'But you agreed to drop me at the house. I paid you in full before we set out!'

'That's right, but all I am saying is that the path gets narrower from this point, and it's difficult to manoeuvre the vehicle over that potholed path in the dark.' Ignoring Uday's protests, the driver got out and stretched. 'Hurry up, Babu. I don't want to be delayed any further. It's not too far from here – a young man like you should be able to cover the distance in ten minutes.'

There was clearly no point in arguing. Uday paid off the rude fellow and heaving the rucksack on his shoulders, he began to trudge towards the house. Things hadn't been going well since he landed at the Indira Gandhi International Airport in New Delhi. First, he had missed the domestic flight to Raipur. Then, the cab drivers at the airport were not willing to go all the way to Bastar. It had taken the promise of double fare and much cajoling for this cab driver to agree to the trip.

His vehicle wasn't in good shape and halfway through the journey, they'd had to stop to change a tyre. To add to Uday's woes, the driver was addicted to tea, and they'd made frequent tea breaks too. It had been an exhausting day, and all he wanted was a hot meal and a comfortable bed to rest his tired limbs. Weighed under the heavy backpack, Uday trudged towards the house.

The moonless night made things murky. He could barely see his way in the darkness. Navigating by the light of his mobile phone, he walked along the deserted path – just as he had done many years ago. The area was familiar, and yet things had changed so much. Both the trees and the undergrowth were denser and more unkempt than he remembered and had crept closer to the path, making the place look eerie and well, a bit creepy. That had not been the case when he last visited the place.

Keshav Roy, whom he called Keshavmama, was Uday's one and only maternal uncle. A bachelor, the good-natured uncle had been a senior officer in the Indian Forest Service, when he had constructed a large house in the Bastar area. He had named it Shantikunj, which meant the haven of peace. Surrounded by sprawling grounds, it had been a wholesome and peaceful place. Greenery had abounded, and the people who lived nearby had been honest and hard-working.

After retirement, he had settled down in the house with a retinue of servants drawn from the local villages. Keshavmama loved nothing better than hosting guests. As a result, Shantikunj was always full of friends, and relatives. It had been

Uday's favourite childhood retreat. Every year, the entire clan descended during the summer vacation. The chatter and laughter of innumerable aunts, uncles, and cousins had resounded and filled the house. Those had been happy times, a world without a care. While the adults had spent time chatting and playing card games, children had romped around the vast grounds.

All that had changed once Uday had gone abroad for further studies, and he'd continued to live there once he'd gotten a job. He'd got busier as time went by, and the occasional trips to India had become rarer after his parents, who had settled in Kolkata, passed away. Soon, he'd lost touch with all his relatives including his uncle.

Things had continued to be hectic at work, and the long-planned trip to India had been indefinitely delayed, till he received a letter from Keshavmama.

Dear Uday,

It's been a long time since you visited your mama. A lot of things have changed around this place. I am an old man now. You have always been my favourite nephew and I wanted to discuss an important matter with you. Can you take some time off from your work to visit me? Please consider this an urgent request and come as soon as possible.

Yours lovingly,
Keshav mama

Perhaps the old man wants to make a will, Uday had thought at first. Not that he was interested in inheriting the vast property – it would be difficult to maintain while living in the

US. Yet, mama's request was impossible to ignore and so, Uday had begun to make travel plans. *It'll be nice to relax in the quiet of Shantikunj*, he thought. Life had been too frenzied, and he needed a break. Besides, it would give him the opportunity to catch up with Keshavmama and enjoy some family gossip. *Perhaps Keshavmama may even be able to arrange a family reunion so I can meet all our relatives too.*

But despite many attempts, the demands of his job kept him from undertaking the journey. It was several weeks before he took off to India. Since there were no direct flights to the place, the journey to Bastar proved long drawn out and exhausting. There were fresh challenges at every stage. *I am not coming here again, any time soon*, he decided. *Instead, I will invite Keshavmama to visit Silicon Valley. He's sure to enjoy the trip.*

As Uday walked along the meandering dirt track, it began to pour. Cursing the weather, lack of electricity, and the cab driver, he continued along the now slushy path, the light of his phone getting weaker as he neared his destination. The wicket-fenced house, surrounded by giant peepul, mango, and banyan trees, was in complete darkness. The smells of the forest tickled his nostrils, bringing hundreds of childhood memories flooding into his mind.

He sighed. The scraped shins, stolen fruits, and pranks – they'd spent so many carefree days in Shantikunj. Uday recalled the long treks with his cousins through the jungle, climbing trees and going on countless adventures, as he walked along the path. He remembered the happy times spent with his umpteen relatives, some loving and some cranky. From meeting dozens of uncles, aunts, and cousins to the feasts and celebrations, he had enjoyed it all.

Keshavmama had always been an excellent host. A jovial and generous man, he'd always helped all those who'd turned to him in times of need. According to Uday's mother, many unscrupulous relatives and friends had unfortunately exploited the poor man. As he trudged along, he got to thinking about his various uncles and aunts. Since Uday had lost touch with everyone, there had been no opportunity to attend any of the family functions or listen to the gossip thereafter.

Soaked to the skin, the young man hastened towards the house. He could barely make out the outline of the once impressive double-storied house with its interesting nooks and crannies that provided excellent hiding places during his childhood. He had so much fun playing hide and seek with the cousins. As he neared the house, he was surprised to see the dilapidated condition of the once-imposing metal gate. It swayed drunkenly on broken hinges as he pushed it open and walked into the grounds. Uday strained his eyes to locate the entrance to the house. He remembered it as an impressively carved mahogany door with its ornate brass knocker with the lion-head. Smiling as he imagined the expression on his uncle's face, he rapped on the knocker.

After what seemed like at least ten minutes of knocking, Bhurakaka, the elderly factotum, stood gaping at him. Holding the candle aloft, the old retainer stared at the young visitor. Uday had wanted to surprise Keshavmama, so he had arrived unannounced.

'Kaka, it's me – Uday! Don't you recognize me?' Uday wanted to hug the old man who had been around the place ever since the house was constructed.

The old man was taken aback at this sudden arrival. Bhurakaka seemed to find his tongue at last. 'Uday baba! You have grown into a fine gentleman. But why haven't you visited Shantikunj for so long?'

'Well, I am here now,' Uday said cheerfully. It was nice to be back in Shantikunj. He suddenly realised how much he had missed the place.

'I didn't know you were coming,' he grumbled. 'No one tells me anything, these days.' The years had not been kind to the gaunt man. In the dim light of the candle, Uday could see there were deep lines on the man's face, and he looked hollow-eyed. It was evident from the sunken cheeks, hollow eyes, and frighteningly bony shoulders that Bhura was not in good health. Uday made a mental note to take Bhurakaka to a doctor while he was at Shantikunj.

'Mama is well, I hope,' said Uday as he walked into the hallway.

The hall stood in the centre, with corridors running on either side. Leading Uday towards a room on the left side of the corridor, Bhurakaka said, 'Come this way. I will show you to your room. We didn't know you were coming, and I have not prepared a room for you, but that can wait. In the meantime, you can freshen up before joining the others in the dining hall.'

Uday could hear loud laughter coming from a distance. 'Others? Are there guests in the house?'

'Yes, your mama's friends are here – eleven of them.'

So, it was going to be a full house. The house was big enough to accommodate a large number of people, and the formal dining hall had hosted innumerable gatherings. Uday smiled at the memory of the many parties he had witnessed during his summer vacations here. Keshavmama had had a group of friends who always landed up at Shantikunj to celebrate special occasions and birthdays. The men, mostly bachelors or widowers, were long-time friends of his uncle's.

'Is the power cut likely to last a while?' Uday asked as he followed the old man down the corridor.

'One never knows,' replied Bhurakaka. He ushered Uday into a guest room that had seen better days. 'There is no surety.'

Leaving the candle with him, the old man left the room. Uday washed up as well as he could in the semi-darkness before walking to the dining hall. He heard the guests before he saw them. Walking in, he saw they were all sitting around the enormous dining table laden with food.

The room was dimly lit with two candelabras, each holding a couple of candles, at either end. The candles threw more shadows than light, and Uday could barely discern the features of the people seated in the room. Once his eyes adjusted, he was surprised to see that they were not the usual group of his uncle's friends. This was a motley group of men and women, none of them familiar.

Keshavmama was sitting at the head of the table. 'Uday, you've finally arrived,' he shouted. To the young man's surprise, his uncle made no effort to get up and greet him. The others ignored that he was in the room and continued talking.

'I am sorry I could not come sooner,' Uday apologized. 'Good evening!' He greeted the guests.

'You are too late, but it doesn't matter anymore,' replied Keshavmama. 'Anyway, sit down and join the discussion since you are here.'

Feeling disappointed at the cold greeting, Uday took his seat at the foot of the table. *Have I made a mistake coming all the way*?' he wondered. But he was ravenous after the long day he'd had – all he wanted was to finish dinner and hit the sack. The others, however, didn't seem to be in a hurry, and an animated discussion was in progress.

'We are talking about paranormal things,' said the bespectacled man seated to his right. His face dimly illuminated by the candles, the gaunt man leaned conspiratorially and asked, 'Have you ever encountered a ghost?'

Uday had been party to many similar discussions in his childhood. Drunk on happiness, aided by alcohol, Keshavmama, and his guests had loved nothing more than an animated discussion. Politics, films, literature, art – nothing was off the table.

'I don't believe in ghosts,' Uday said, unwilling to be drawn into the discussion. He was too tired to debate the fanciful subject. 'They only exist in the imagination. I am a data scientist, and I don't indulge in fantasies.'

'Ah, a man with a scientific temperament?' snorted the gentleman. His eyes shining through the spectacles, he said, 'They think they are infallible. Let me warn you, you will change your mind about the supernatural.'

'How can you be sure there are ghosts? Have you seen one?' Uday snapped. He was too tired to play guessing games or take part in pointless discussions.

'Of course, I have seen ghosts. Young man, let me tell you a story. It's something I have experienced – it's not fiction, I assure you.'

'Yes, yes,' clamoured a couple of men. 'A true story is always interesting.'

'I have a story too,' exclaimed a portly fellow seated near the storyteller, keen to grab the spotlight.

It's going to be a long night, Uday thought, sighing as the first story began.

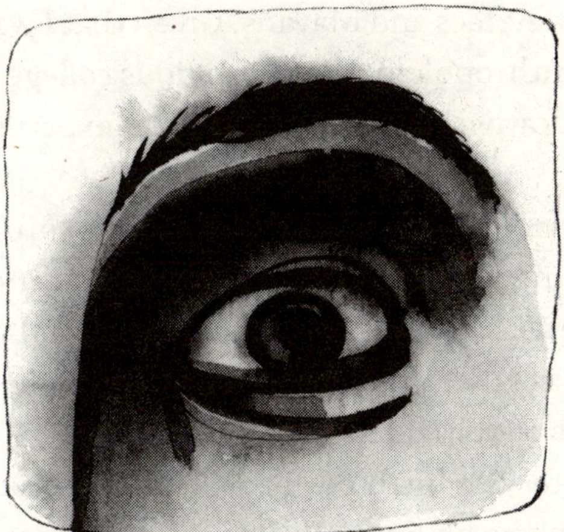

1

THE CREEPY DOLL

'It had been another sleepless night, a sixth consecutive night of madness, in the Bhatnagar home. The nocturnal upheaval left us bleary-eyed and exhausted every morning. We snapped at each other, unable to concentrate on work, dreading the nightmare promised to us each night.

I distinctly remembered the day it began. The three of us—my wife, daughter, and I—had been on a holiday in Mexico.

The Aztec civilization and culture have fascinated me for a long time, and I was keen to absorb the sights and flavours of Mexico. My training as an anthropologist has a lot to do with my interest in Aztecs and Mayans. Given that I was a professor and taught anthropology in a prestigious college, I considered traveling educative. There's nothing like experiencing things in person.

Amrita, my wife, shared my obsession with the reconstructing, interpreting, and understanding of past human societies. She was an archaeologist and taught at the same college as I did. We had travelled quite extensively during the early days of our marriage, but things changed about seven years ago, after the birth of our daughter – Aria's arrival put most of our plans on hold. We had waited many years to take the Mexico trip, and when it finally happened, we wanted to accomplish as much as possible in the fortnight we were there.

We took in the sights, enjoyed Mexican food and music, taking hundreds of pictures and video clips of our experiences. Our interest must have infected Aria too because she enjoyed the trip in her own way.

The Aztec civilization is as interesting as the Egyptian one. When it was finally explored, Teotihuacan turned out to be a treasure trove of ancient structures. Built in around 400 BCE, it is one of the country's oldest archaeological sites. Templo Mayor, the Great Temple, a remnant of the ancient capital, is as majestic now as it must have been in ancient times. The highlight of our trip was our visits to various museums. We spent an entire day inside the National Museum of Anthropology in Mexico City, which is filled with a carefully curated collection of archaeological and Aztec artifacts. Amrita was fascinated by the turquoise and obsidian Aztec masks, the exquisite Shield of Yanhuitlán crafted from gold and turquoise, while I stood rooted before the replica of Codex Borbonicus written by the Aztec priests.

We were a few days from returning home when we met Carmina Martinez, a fellow anthropologist, and friend who taught at the New University of Mexico, for dinner. I'd met her during a global seminar on the Aztec civilization, and we'd hit it off.

'You should spend your last day cruising the canals of Xochimilco, which is a UNESCO World Heritage site. The canals and chinampas—man-made islands—are a tourist favourite,' she laughed. Glancing doubtfully at Aria, she said, 'I don't know whether you should take your daughter, but the Island of Dolls is a very interesting place.'

I'd read about the island and the horrific collection of dolls on it, and I was keen to visit the place. Since we had no place to leave Aria, we decided to take her along.

The next morning, we set out for the chinampas. Our backpacks filled with food and water, we sailed along the Xochimilco canals in the city in a colourful boat called a trajinera, which reminded me of the shikaras of Srinagar. There were three other people in our boat, one of them an enthusiastic young Australian journalist in search of an interesting story and a polite Japanese couple. With us was also our talkative local guide named Alvaro. The gloomy semi-darkness of the overcast day seemed to cast a spell over the group as he spoke.

'We must walk around the Island of Dolls,' Alvaro said. 'It would be a tragedy to miss the place.'

It was a relaxing cruise as the trajinera meandered around the labyrinthine canals surrounded by lush greenery. The journey was as beautiful and serene as described by Carmina. All of a sudden, our progress slowed, and a hush fell. Our boat turned around a bend in the canal, and someone screamed. It was the Japanese lady in the boat. I looked around, on the island in the distance were hundreds of dolls hanging from trees. It was a very distressing sight, sending shivers down my spine. Nothing I read about the island had prepared me for such a sight.

Worried, I looked at Amrita, who seemed stricken. She tried to divert Aria's attention, but the girl seemed mesmerized by the sight. She loved dolls and had a sizeable collection at home. The journalist jumped out of the boat and shouted excitedly, clicking countless pictures. The Japanese couple sat in the boat, numb and reluctant to get out. After a few moments of indecision, and after the guide had brought the boat onto the bank, they got up and followed him to the island.

I was wondering if we should remain in the boat when Alvaro beckoned to us. We got off and followed him, averting our gaze from the surrounding horror. The mutilated dolls with missing heads and limbs, and blank eyes, hanging from trees, fences, and every imaginable place, were a disturbing sight. Large, small, and tiny – dolls of all sizes hung from the trees.

Covered in spider webs, these dolls were terrifying in their weirdness. A few had been decapitated, and only the heads were now hanging from various branches. To my horror, the empty eye sockets and open mouths were swarming with large insects of some strange species. The creatures had taken refuge inside the dolls' hollow bodies – it was a sight from a nightmare.

'Long ago, this *chinampa* belonged to a man called Don Julián Santana Barrera,' said Alvaro softly. His voice sounded creepy as he continued, 'He built a shack here and lived all alone. One day, he found the body of a young girl floating in the canal. He also found a doll floating near her. Barrera buried the girl's body on the island. He was a superstitious man, and he thought that the dead girl would be lonely without the doll, and so he hung it from a tree near his shack.'

I was not interested in the story because I'd read all about it on the internet. All I wanted was to get Aria out of that place, while others listened to the guide.

'But strange things began to happen after Barrera hung the doll from the tree. He started hearing the girl's screams, and footsteps sounded outside his shack every night. Soon, the entire place was filled with the sound of whispers and moaning,' Alvaro continued as we traipsed through the island. 'Barrera went crazy – he was convinced that the dead girl's ghost wanted the company of some more dolls, and he started collecting dolls and hanging them from the trees, wire fence, and wherever he found any space. He continued to do so for the next fifty years.'

'But why are the heads and limbs missing?' the Japanese lady asked. She seemed so upset that she refused to look up from the ground. 'The decapitated dolls look *ghastly*!'

'Barrera was so frightened of the girl's spirit that he began collecting dolls from wherever he could. Sometimes he got them from the trash and sometimes from the canal. Do you know there are more than *1,500* dolls on this island?' Alvaro exclaimed, waving his hands around. 'Anyway, he continued living on the island and hanging dolls everywhere until he died in 2001. Strangely, he was found floating in the same canal, and it is said in the same spot, where he found the dead girl and her doll.'

There was stunned silence as we tried to imagine the life of a crazy man surrounded by hundreds of mutilated dolls.

'Are there ghosts on the island?' Aria piped up. She had an imaginative mind, and the gruesome sight of the dolls was clearly giving her ideas.

'People believe there are ghosts on this island,' Alvaro smiled. 'Many tourists bring dolls and hang them from trees here, hoping their wishes come true. People also leave donations at the doll shrine,' the guide hinted, but none of us obliged him. We had already paid a hefty fee for his services.

'I want to leave a doll here,' Aria tugged at Amrita's hand.

'All right, my dear, we'll bring a doll when we come here the next time,' her mother promised.

A pretty doll, which had been left at the base of a tree by a visitor not too long ago, arrested Aria's attention. Most of its limbs were intact, and it didn't have the weathered look of most of the other dolls. 'I want that doll,' said Aria.

'No, darling, we can't take that one, but I'll get you a new one,' Amrita promised the child.

'Please don't touch or remove any doll from its resting place,' Alvaro warned, noticing Aria's interest.

'We have no intention of touching anything,' I retorted icily. 'Can we please go back now?'

'As soon as everyone is ready to leave,' said the guide.

Everyone was ready to leave, except the journalist, who had wandered off to take some more pictures. There was nothing to do but wait for the fellow to return. In the meantime, I tried to distract my daughter as best as I could. It was a while before he returned, and I heaved a sigh of relief.

Silently, we made our way back to the shore. Physically exhausted and emotionally drained, we spent the rest of the evening ruminating about the spooky island.

The next day, brushing off the only unpleasant part of our Mexico sojourn, the three of us embarked on our return flight to India.

Our troubles began soon after we reached home when Amrita discovered the doll in Aria's backpack. '*Why*? Why would you take it?' she cried, shaking the child. 'Don't we buy you enough?'

'Her name's Juana,' Aria replied. 'When I was on the island, she whispered to me, asking me to take her home. Juana told me she wants to live with us.'

'Are you crazy? Dolls don't whisper.'

I was aghast when I heard what Aria had to say. A strange foreboding seized my heart as I looked at the doll. It seemed to stare back at me in a creepy manner, its eyes strangely alive and full of scorn.

'We should throw the doll away,' I said that night when Amrita joined me in our bedroom. 'I am not comfortable with it in the house.'

'The guide had warned us against carrying any dolls away,' she frowned. 'I don't know how or when Aria tucked it into her backpack.'

'What's done is done. Let's just throw it away now.'

'Aria is sleeping with it, and it will be tough to take it away from her,' Amrita whispered. 'I will throw it out when she's at school.'

And that's what we did the next morning. The doll was duly dumped in the garbage bin, which was taken away by the cleaners. We heaved a sigh of relief.

That evening, Aria was distressed when she couldn't find the doll. We feigned ignorance and promised to buy a set of new Barbie dolls to make up for the loss, but she was inconsolable. 'I want Juana,' she cried.

That night, we had barely gone to sleep when an unexpected storm hit the city. The doors and windows started to bang open and shut. A strong gale almost broke the front door down. It suddenly flew open, and all the lights went out.

'Didn't you latch the door?' I shouted above the din of the storm.

'I did,' said Amrita, her voice sounding disembodied in the dark. 'It must be the storm. Why don't you latch it again?'

Carrying a torch, I walked slowly towards the door when I saw the doll standing on the doorstep, the size of a human being. I dropped my torch, rooted to the spot. The doll began to laugh, an evil sound emanating from its mouth.

'Did you really think you could get rid of me?' it smirked. Its eyes were red, as if raining fire.

Amrita heard the laughter and came to join me at the door. She shrieked and collapsed to the ground. Immobilized with fear, I continued standing by the door. Its mocking laughter continued to ring around the house as the doll entered Aria's bedroom at the end of the corridor.

Terrified at what may happen, I rushed into Aria's bedroom behind the doll. To my horror and amazement, I saw that the doll had now reverted to its former size and was lying next to my daughter. But a strange thing happened when I tried to remove it from Aria's side. It remained there, as if glued to the spot.

My mind was in turmoil as I walked down to our room. Amrita had recovered a little and now lay sobbing on the bed. 'What will we do?' she wailed.

I took her in my arms and stroked her hair softly. 'We'll think of something – don't worry,' I comforted her. But I did not know what we could do.

The garbage dump was many kilometres away, and yet the doll had found its way back to our house. *The next time, we will drive a longer distance off to throw it away*, I decided.

Two days later, while Aria was at school, Amrita and I drove towards the ghats between Pune and Mumbai with the doll in the back seat. We drove about 130 kilometres away to find a ridge on the highway. Then, we tossed the doll into a ravine. Rubbing our hands with satisfaction, we drove back just in time for Aria to return from school.

When she discovered the doll missing, our daughter threw a tantrum. 'Where is Juana?' she demanded angrily.

'Isn't the doll in your bedroom?' Amrita countered.

'I know you've been trying to get rid of her – she's told me everything. But your plans won't work. Juana will return and punish the two of you,' Aria warned.

True to her prediction, the doll was back in Aria's bedroom that night, and with her return began a series of horrific incidents that threw our lives into chaos. All of a sudden, unexpected accidents began to take place. First, Amrita fell down the stairs and fractured her leg. 'Somebody pushed me down the stairs,' she insisted. 'It's lucky I didn't break my back. That doll is evil – we *have* to get rid of it.'

The next day, the gas stove in the kitchen was turned on by invisible hands, and the whole thing caught fire. I burned my hands trying to put it off, and we just about escaped a major disaster. And a couple of days later, a sudden fire ruined the wooden gate to our house.

It was clear that we were in for a bad time. A series of unexplained short circuits damaged some of our gadgets. The bathroom taps suddenly turned on, flooding the bedrooms. Bizarre, almost fatal, accidents took place around our house. It was all too frightening, and we did not know what to do.

As I tried to find a way to get rid of the doll, a strange change suddenly came over Aria. From a compassionate and kind-hearted girl who treated her dolls with the utmost care, she turned violent. We found her pulling off the limbs, removing the eyeballs and tearing out the hair of her dolls. She also began to hurt animals and behave terribly with her friends. Aria began using curse words we never used at home. Soon, we began getting complaints from her teachers. Aria had pulled a girl's hair, bitten a boy, and scratched another one's face. She was exhibiting signs of unexpected viciousness. It was all very uncharacteristic of our daughter, who was a gentle and friendly soul.

Finally, it was the school principal who suggested we should consult Mrs Joseph, the school counsellor.

Mrs Joseph was an experienced counsellor. She had several sessions with our daughter, talking to her about various things. Surprisingly, not once did Aria mention anything about the doll. For a while, everything seemed to be going right before it slipped back into the same problems with fresh complaints about Aria's violent behaviour.

After a few weeks, Mrs Joseph gave up, and the principal requested us to keep Aria away from the school until she was better. We met Mrs Joseph and tried to find a way out of the mess. 'I think the child had a traumatic experience, which is leading to the streak of violence. There is little I can do in the matter,' she said. 'I tried my best, but it's not working. I suggest you consult a professional child psychiatrist for a solution.'

'You mean a psychiatrist?' The suggestion appalled us.

'There's nothing wrong with consulting a psychiatrist,' said the counsellor. 'Many parents consult a psychiatrist when their child starts behaving in an abnormal manner. Aria has been with us for three years, and we know she's friendly and well-behaved. There must be a reason for this unusual behaviour. What she needs is professional handling. You should go see Dr Kalpana Nair – she's a renowned expert, and I am sure she'll be able to help you.'

The counsellor then gave us the psychiatrist's contact details and offered to fix up an appointment.

Back at home, Amrita and I discussed the matter. Things were definitely getting out of control. We couldn't allow Aria's schooling to suffer – it was time to consult the psychiatrist.

Dr Nair turned out to be a gentle and experienced person. She spoke with our daughter. It was a week before she finally spoke to us.

'Aria seems a well-brought up girl. If she has become violent, there *must* be a reason,' she said. 'Please tell me everything that has taken place in your family in the last six months.'

Amrita told the doctor everything, including our trip to Mexico, after which our lives had taken this strange turn. We told her about the doll and the incidents that had taken place thereafter. She listened to our story and was silent for a few minutes. We realized it was an incredible story, which she seemed to find hard to believe.

'I think the horror Aria witnessed on the Island of Dolls is preying on her psyche – it seems to have left a lasting impression on her mind,' said Dr Nair. 'You shouldn't have taken her there. It's not a place meant for impressionable children. It will take her time to get over the experience, and the doll is a constant reminder. It must be removed from your house.'

We then told her about our attempts to throw the doll and the ensuing reactions.

'I don't know how you can get rid of the doll, but it has to be done for your daughter to get over the trauma,' Dr Nair advised.

But Amrita and I knew that it was easier said than done.

I was now at my wit's end. As a last resort, I finally called Carmina and told her the entire story. Although I had spoken to her after returning from Mexico, I had not shared what had happened with the doll, and she was shocked when I did.

'The doll is ruining our lives,' I said, breaking down. 'Amrita and I have not known a moment's peace since it came to our house. You *have* to help me find a solution.'

'Be strong, Arindam,' Carmina said, her voice filled with concern. 'I think you must come back to Mexico. The only way to get rid of the doll is to leave it where it belongs. Your daughter made the mistake of removing it from the island, and your family is now paying the price for the folly.'

Since I had already been thinking along similar lines, her suggestion was an endorsement of the idea.

'I will meet you at the airport whenever you arrive, and we'll go to the island together,' Carmina said. 'Meanwhile, I will speak to Alvaro, the guide who took you to the island. We *will* handle the issue.'

I began applications for a visa, which took some time to arrive, and then I embarked on this mission. I left home before Aria was awake. Fearful that the doll would give me the slip, I tucked it in my hand baggage and kept a close watch over it all through the journey. As promised, my Carmina was waiting at the airport. She drove me straight to the trajinera boarding point, where we met Alvaro. With the doll still safe in my backpack, the three of us set out for the island.

'I warned you not to pick up any dolls, amigo,' Alvaro said, unable to resist the opportunity to rebuke me. 'The dolls on that island are restless spirits. They do not spare anyone.'

'That's all right, Alvaro!' Carmina said, trying to pacify the man. 'Their daughter took the doll without their knowledge. She loves dolls, and this specific doll seems to have whispered to her. Children find it difficult to resist toys. It was a mistake, of course.'

We cruised silently along the canal. I was terribly anxious about putting the doll back in its original place. The sooner we got rid of the devil, the better it was. Soon, we reached the Island of Dolls. Alvaro led me to a tree, and I hung the doll from a branch, but it fell to the ground. I tried several times, but each time it would fall.

'This isn't the right place,' Alvaro declared. He led me to another tree, and I repeated the process, but the doll continued to fall to the ground. We tried several trees with the same result. By the time we reached the seventh tree that the guide pointed out, I was emotionally exhausted. But this time, I was successful. The doll remained on the branch, dangling and swaying as though rejoicing in her return to the island.

I felt her chuckling and heard the whispers from the dolls dangling around her. They seemed to be welcoming their friend home. The experience was too creepy for words. I felt myself collapsing and would have fallen if Alvaro's strong arms hadn't supported me into the boat. It was only after I landed in India that I could relax.

Relieved at finally getting rid of the doll, I slept for the next twenty-four hours straight. I could sense a change as soon as I woke up. There was a sense of peace that had been missing since Aria had carried the doll home. Aria returned to her former self, going back to school with no complaints. Her violent behaviour vanished as suddenly as it had appeared. There were no more creepy events in our house either.

A few days later, I sat in our living room with my wife and shared the details of my journey to Mexico. I told her how Carmina and Alvaro felt that the spooky incidents were connected with the evil doll and had helped me get rid of it.' Arindam took off his spectacles and cleaned them with a handkerchief. His hands were shaky, Uday noticed. There was no doubt that he had suffered deeply, and telling the story seemed to bring him peace.

There was an eerie silence as the audience came to terms with the horrifying tale.

'That was a very interesting and spooky story,' the portly man said, nodding. 'I have heard of the Island of Dolls, but never met someone who's been there.'

'Do you think everyone who visits the island would have a spooky experience?' Uday's question was laced with disbelief. It would take a lot more than a story to convince him about the presence of spooky entities in the world.

'Well, I refuse to debate that point.' The curt response came from the narrator. 'Why don't you visit the island and find an answer?'

The sarcastic comment brought forth an amused snort from another guest.

2

TOO LATE FOR REGRETS

'It's my turn now,' the portly guest rubbed his hands gleefully at the prospect of regaling the others. 'I am going to tell a story everyone in the room will like.' Clearing his throat, he continued, 'By the way, the protagonist's father is a close friend, so I know it's a true story.'

'Well, get on with it,' said Keshavmama.

'The story is about a young man named Atul who worked in a tea estate. He had been happy and content till that fateful morning when I will begin the story. The tea garden, with its lush green surroundings, had failed to comfort Atul that morning. It had never happened in the last nineteen years of living in the tea estate in the foothills of the Himalayas. The undulating terrain, covered in a green tapestry of varying shades, the silvery mist, and the smiling faces around him, had never failed to bring cheer to his heart.

That morning, he stared at the faraway hills, sipping the first flush Darjeeling tea, wondering if things would get better. Nineteen years! It seemed a lifetime since he had begun working at the Greenview Tea Estate as junior estate manager. But Atul was a fast learner. Within the first two years, he had learned everything about the estate and knew each worker by name. Girish Agarwal, the plantation owner, was a skilful and generous man, and he had liked Atul. In fact, he had trusted him. Soon, he had begun to involve Atul in all aspects of running the estate. As a result, within six years, Atul had found himself promoted to estate manager.

Like most tea estates in Darjeeling, the Greenview Tea Estate had once belonged to an Englishman. It changed hands several times after independence till Agarwal bought the sprawling estate. All had not been well at the tea plantations when he bought the estate. Rains had been erratic, and productivity had suffered, with the losses mounting. As a result, most workers had moved to greener pastures. But Agarwal was not one to give up. He had invested in new machinery and introduced several welfare measures for workers to attract them back to the estate. The promise of better wages and incentives drew them back, and it was during that phase that Atul had joined the estate.

The two of them had decided to undo the damage to the estate. It had taken them four years to turn things around, and soon the estate began to flourish. Things were going well for Atul. He was a cheerful and hardworking young man who was respected and trusted by the workers. A confirmed bachelor from Kolkata, he was the only son of a professor. It had always been his dream to be the manager of a tea estate, and he was now living that dream.

Once he was promoted as the estate manager, Atul was allotted a large colonial bungalow surrounded by tea gardens, which had a stunning view of the snow-clad mountains around him. The picturesque bungalow, equipped with Victorian furniture, fireplace, and trappings, had once belonged to an Englishman, and living in it was like living in the previous century. Besides, the air was pure and the environs beautiful.

Atul could not have asked for more – everything was going well; the workers were happy, and the tea they produced fetched a good price. But not long after, Girish Agarwal fell ill, and his doctors advised him to go to Kolkata for surgery. He was told to remain there until he had fully recovered. Realizing that his days of actively participating in the business were over, Girish had decided to retire, and the management of the estate was passed on to Vikram, his eldest son. The swashbuckling and ambitious fellow had studied management abroad. His ideas about business differed vastly from his father's. While Girish Agarwal believed in keeping the staff and workers happy in order to motivate them to be better at their work, his son wanted to cut costs and maximize profits in the shortest time possible. He was an impatient man, waiting to prove his credentials.

Tea auctions have, traditionally, been the main way for tea producers to sell their wares. Every year, they gathered at one of the seven auction centres in the country, where they found bulk buyers for their tea.

That year, Vikram and Atul attended the auction in Kolkata. Atul had attended several auctions with Girish Agarwal, but it was the first time for Vikram. The experience turned out to be a major fiasco. That year, because of poor weather, the productivity and quality of tea had been far from satisfactory. Vikram was disappointed with the price offered for Greenview Estate tea. He had expected his garden produce to fetch the best price at the auction.

He looked accusingly at Atul and asked, 'Shouldn't we have gotten a better price? You have been telling me that the tea from our gardens is the best in the area.'

'The quality and quantity of tea vary each year. The weather has an important role to play in the matter. We have done our best, but the weather in not in our control,' replied Atul, Vikram's behaviour irking him.

'You have failed to deliver the goods. I don't think your best is good enough for the estate,' Vikram said as he strode away, leaving Atul staring at his back.

Atul tried to catch up and explain, but the young owner continued to blame him.

Vikram went back to Darjeeling in a foul mood. It took Atul a couple of days to finish all the paperwork and return to Greenview. He was surprised to find his office locked. He wondered if Vikram had declared a holiday, but the other rooms in the office complex were open.

He was about to ask the peon when he saw Vikram walking towards his plush office.

'What are you doing here?' asked Vikram.

His question surprised Atul. 'I don't understand ...' he began.

'Have you not checked your email?' Vikram interrupted.

Atul took out his mobile phone and refreshed his mailbox. There was an email from Vikram. The estate manager could not believe his eyes. The note had just two brief sentences: 'Your services have been terminated because of poor performance. Your accounts will be promptly settled.'

And just like that, nineteen years at the tea garden had come to an abrupt end. Atul knew it was futile to reason with his new boss. Feeling hurt by how Vikram had rewarded his hard work and loyalty, he walked back to his bungalow.

He sat down on the easy chair laid out on the veranda and brooded over what to do next. Atul called out to the cook, Gurung, and asked for a cup of tea. The cook, who did not know that Atul had been sacked, was surprised to see him return to the bungalow so soon.

'You are not feeling well, sahib?' Gurung asked, thinking the estate manager looked unwell. 'Shall I call the doctor?'

'I am all right, Gurung, just a little headache. No need to call the doctor.'

His mind was turbulent as he sat sipping tea, for once the sight of the lush green tea gardens and the distant mountains failed to cheer him up. He knew that any of the tea estates would willingly employ him, but he loved the Greenview Tea

Estate. In the past nineteen years, he had established a good relationship with the workers. The sudden dismissal from his employer had jolted Atul.

'Sahib,' Gurung said, holding a tray with an envelope on it. 'There's a letter for you.'

Atul knew it was more bad news. Vikram was determined to make a scapegoat of him for the low tea prices at the auction. He opened the letter slowly. It was a notice to vacate the bungalow within three days, designed to be a blow to his ego. It was the ultimate humiliation. There would be no farewells or speeches, no acknowledgement of his loyalty and hard work.

I won't stay another moment, Atul decided. He called Gurung and asked him to pack all his belongings.

'Are you going somewhere, sahib?' The simple Gorkha had been working for Atul for all of his time at the estate. He was taken aback at the sudden changes that had taken place since morning. Something was drastically wrong. He had never seen Atul sahib in such a grim mood – not even during the worst of times.

'I am going to Kolkata, Gurung,' said Atul sadly.

'When will you return, sahib?'

'I don't know.' Atul didn't have the heart to share the sad news with this loyal man.

An hour later, his car was packed and ready. Atul called his gardener and Gurung. 'Thank you for making my stay comfortable. I can never repay you for your love, but here's a token of my appreciation.' Hugging them by turns, he gave them 5,000 rupees each.

It was a tearful farewell. The two men could not believe that their sahib would not be returning to the bungalow. The wizened gardener wiped away his tears on his sleeves, saying, 'I am sure you will return. You love the estate too much.'

Atul's eyes misted over, but he smiled.

'Take me with you, sahib,' pleaded Gurung. 'I don't want money.'

'No, Gurung! You must continue to work at the bungalow. I am sure a new manager will arrive very soon,' said Atul. 'He'll need your services.'

It was 10.30 a.m. when Atul cast one last look at the tea estate. He didn't want to cause any complications by meeting the workers and staff. Steeling himself, he drove out of the estate gates. He topped up the tank at the first petrol pump and headed for Kolkata.

Back in his office, Vikram was glad to have Atul out of his way. The estate manager had long been an obstacle. At the top of his agenda was cutting costs and improving the quality of tea from the gardens. He wanted to get rid of the flab and turn the estate into a lean and efficient one. Atul had protested when he wanted to sack the old staff and workers.

'We can't take their jobs away, Vikram,' he had said. "Those workers have worked hard for the estate. They have been here since your father's time, and Greenview is their only source of income. The least we should do is compensate them properly for terminating their services.'

'Things can't continue the way they were in my father's time – we have been paying too much for the workers. A lot of money is being wasted on welfare measures because those won't improve the quality of the tea. Those methods of motivation are outdated, and I have decided to revamp the entire system,' Vikram declared.

Atul's protests had no effect on Vikram, and he made a list of the employees whose services had to be terminated. With the estate manager gone, he would have no difficulty in implementing his plans. He began taking immediate action. The first thing he did was to take over the duties of the estate manager as soon as Atul left and redeploy the workforce. Since he believed that the young and energetic could do a better job, he set about sacking the old and experienced workers. The news that Atul had left the estate spread rapidly among the workers.

The staff and tea garden workers were aghast. No one liked Vikram Agarwal. His arrogant behaviour and newfangled methods irritated the employees. By noon, word about the sacking of the senior workers had also spread through the estate. It brought uncertainty to every worker. Would I be the next to be sacked, they wondered. The ones who had lost jobs were not about to give up easily. Their families would go hungry if they didn't find a job and it was not easy to find employment in the region. The sacked workers decided to sit in dharna. They demanded compensation for the termination of their services and pleaded with other workers to join their protest. 'This could happen to you tomorrow,' they appealed.

Soon, the other workers joined the dharna, and work came to a standstill. The younger, more rebellious workers threatened Vikram with dire consequences.

In the meantime, Atul had reached Siliguri. It was 1.30 p.m, and he had been driving for three hours and needed a break. So, he stopped at a dhaba for lunch. He knew it was not possible to reach Kolkata that day. Night fell suddenly in the hills, and it was not safe to negotiate the steep and treacherous bends after dark.

While he was waiting for his food to be served, Atul took out his mobile phone and consulted the map for a suitable place to spend the night. Raiganj, which was about 125 kilometres away, would be a good place, he realized. He could reach there before dark. Once that was done, he called Girish Agarwal. He felt dutybound to share this news with the man who had been a father figure to him.

As expected, Girish Agarwal was shocked to hear that Atul had been sacked.

'Don't go to Kolkata, Atul. Please turn back immediately – I will speak to Vikram right away,' he said. 'Greenview needs you, son,' the old man pleaded.

'Sir, please don't embarrass me,' Atul said. 'I have great respect for you. However, I have been dismissed by Vikram. I will return only if he asks me to do so. We have to work as a team, and any resentment will not be good for the estate.'

Ten minutes later, Girish Agarwal gave his son an earful. 'How *dare* you sack the man who turned our estate around? Mark my words, the estate will go down the hill in no time. Don't you realize that your ideas have no place in running a tea estate? Those may appear good in theory but are not practical. I want you to apologize to Atul and request him to return immediately.'

But Vikram was adamant, and he refused to heed his father's advice. 'I won't beg Atul to return. We don't need him. Don't worry, Papa, I will take care of everything,' he promised. 'I will appoint an efficient estate manager, and you will see the improvements in both quality and production levels.'

Nothing Girish said could change his son's mind. It was futile to argue with the hot-headed fellow, Girish realized. The estate he had nurtured painstakingly was clearly headed for disaster.

Atul had decided that he would not return unless Vikram apologized. But Vikram neither called nor sent a message. Atul knew that the young man was too proud to apologize to a mere employee. Shrugging, he continued to Raiganj.

Back at the estate, in a couple of days, Vikram had found things spinning out of control. The striking workers refused to return to work until he compensated the workers who had been terminated. But even that didn't work, and resentment continued to brew within the workforce. Many of the good workers migrated to other tea gardens.

As a result, production began to fall, and the quality of tea suffered. The prime orthodox tea was worse than the CTC variety. Vikram saw that he had placed wrong people in the wrong place. In the absence of an able leader, the workers were a demotivated lot. Most of them were dispirited and shirked responsibilities. They had no respect nor love for the ruthless young owner. Vikram did not know whom to depend upon and felt totally isolated.

By the end of two weeks, Vikram knew he had to abandon his ego. He emailed Atul, requesting him to return to the estate. *The estate is in dire straits*, he wrote, *I need your expertise to bring things back to the former state. Greenview Tea Estate needs you.*

Atul was distraught. He loved the estate and he was upset at the news that Greenview Tea Estate was going downhill. Vikram's appeal worked, and Atul was soon back at work. As soon as he arrived at the estate, Atul realised things had gone horribly out of control. It would take months of patience and hard work to bring the production to the previous level. He set about working without wasting any time. The workers were happy to see the friendly estate manager going around the tea gardens, motivating the workers, and inspecting the factory.

Vikram gave Atul a free hand in running the estate. Relaxed after handing over the reins to capable hands, he left for his long pending holiday abroad.

The first thing Atul did was to bring back the old and experienced workers, resulting in a visible difference in the attitude of the workers. They were happy again. Under Atul's supervision and motivation, they resumed working hard. Soon, things started looking up in the Greenview Tea Estate. Slowly and steadily, productivity began rising, and the quality of the produce also improved.

After returning from his holiday, Vikram was impressed by the changes in the tea estate. He decided to invite Atul for dinner at his bungalow, but the estate manager excused himself on some pretext or the other each time Vikram's secretary tried to fix a day. Although Vikram spoke over the phone, he never got to meet Atul. In fact, the young man hardly ever sat at his desk. He was always out supervising the garden workers.

He is still smarting, so he must be avoiding me, Vikram thought. *I'll give him some more time.*

Several months passed, and things were much better at the Greenview Tea Estate. It was then that Girish Agarwal decided to spend the summer at the tea garden. He was happy that Vikram had learned his lesson, and Atul was in charge of the estate. He flew into Bagdogra Airport, spent the day with a friend, and after lunch and some tea, he drove to Darjeeling. It was dark by the time he reached Greenview.

Vikram was surprised to see his father sitting in his bungalow when he returned from work late that evening.

'I've been waiting for you,' said Girish. 'Let's go to the estate manager's bungalow. I want to meet Atul and thank him for the turnaround at Greenview.'

'I will take you there,' Vikram offered. By this time, he had realized Atul's worth, but he couldn't swallow his ego and express his gratitude. But he wanted to do so now, with his father by his side. 'I owe him thanks too.'

They walked to the bungalow, which was completely dark. They could see no one. 'Where is Atul? The bungalow looks deserted. Doesn't he live here anymore?' Girish asked his son.

'I really don't know,' Vikram said, looking surprised. He had maintained a discreet distance from the estate manager. 'He may have just moved off the estate.'

'That's sad, Vicky. Atul is a good man and deserves better treatment. You've been harsh to someone who's done much for this estate. He rejected several offers, some with better prospects, because he loved this estate. Do you realize he has been with us for almost twenty years now?'

Vikram looked sheepish, knowing that his father was right. He had not bothered to find out if Atul was living in the bungalow, and the staff had not informed him either. The staff and workers did not like Vikram, and they shared no information with the impetuous man.

'I want you to find out where he's living – do it right now. Call and invite him to dinner,' Girish said, turning to walk towards Vikram's bungalow, his son at his heels.

'I tried to invite him to dinner a couple of times, but he made excuses,' Vikram grumbled. 'He seems to be avoiding me.'

'I am not surprised,' said Girish. 'Atul will not refuse my invitation. Try and find him.'

Back at his bungalow, Vikram went into action immediately. He sent a few people to look for Atul at the guest houses around the area and made phone calls to the hotels in town. But Atul was not in any of them. Surprised, he asked the watchman and called up a few staff members, but no one knew Atul's whereabouts.

'It's a weekend, Atul might have gone to Kolkata,' Vikram finally said to his father.

'He is not irresponsible like that – he wouldn't leave without informing you!' Girish was puzzled.

'There must have been an emergency,' Vikram said, trying to find an explanation.

'Call him even if he's left for Kolkata,' Girish said, raising his voice. 'Tell him I want to meet him.'

After several attempts to call Atul, Vikram turned to his father and said, 'His phone is unreachable, but perhaps his phone ran out of charge.'

'Call his father in Kolkata – his number is listed in my old diary, which is in the study.'

Vikram checked the telephone diary and called Atul's father. Mr Chatterjee had retired from his job as a professor in the University of Calcutta. He now lived in Salt Lake with his wife.

'Hello?'

'Good evening, sir,' Vikram greeted Atul's father. 'I am calling from the Greenview Tea Estate. May I speak to Atul, please?'

'You want to speak to Atul?' asked the old man, sounding surprised at the request. 'Who are you, and what is this about?'

'Well, sir, my name is Vikram Agarwal, my father is here for a couple of days and wants to meet him. Unfortunately, he left without informing anyone. Isn't he in Kolkata?' There was a dead silence at the other end. 'Sir? Are you still on the line?' asked Vikram.

This time, there was a response. 'I am surprised that you do not know that he is no more.' Mr Chatterjee's voice was heavy with grief.

'Atul is *no more*?' Vikram repeated. His brain refused to work. Perplexed, he looked at his father.

Girish Agarwal was looking equally shocked. For eight months, Vikram had claimed that Atul had returned to work and things had improved. He cast a doubtful look at his son. Was he making a fool of him? All those improvements! How had they taken place? Something was wrong.

'But how can that be?' Vikram almost shouted into the phone.

'Atul died eight months ago in a road accident while driving down to Kolkata.'

'That's not possible!'

'Well, son, he died the day you sacked him. His last call was from Siliguri just before he took to the road again. He met with an accident twenty kilometres from Siliguri – he died instantaneously.'

How was it possible? Having spent almost a month in Spain and Portugal, Vikram had been too busy with the visit of his college friends to be involved in the everyday running of the estate. There had been several house guests and parties which left him with little time to interact with Atul. But he had spoken to him almost every second day. Not just that, he had invited him to dinner too.

Guilty and pale, he stammered. 'I am sorry, sir.'

'What's the point of being sorry now? I have lost my son. He can't be brought to life by your remorse,' Mr Chatterjee said, hanging up before Vikram could react.

'Atul loved the tea estate,' Girish whispered and shook his head sadly, his shoulders sagging hopelessly. 'He will continue to haunt this place forever. He has been taking care of the tea gardens for the past eight months. It's sad that you failed to recognize the worth of that man.'

For once, Vikram remained silent. He found no words to express his regret.'

The narrator ended his story and looked around for reactions.

3

THE AIRPORT

'That's a great story! I don't know why people assume all ghosts are unkind and scary,' commented Keshavmama. Uday noticed that he was the first to applaud.

'My story has some interesting elements,' said a gaunt man seated by his uncle's side. 'Would you like me to tell it to you?'

'Yes, yes!' several voices urged.

Uday yawned tiredly as the third man began his story.

'It was an important day in Bengaluru city. The spanking new international airport was ready to receive its first flight. It was almost 10.30 p.m., and the airport wore a festive look, a palpable excitement in the air. A crowd of airport employees, all of whom had worked hard to get the airport ready, had gathered to watch the inaugural flight touch down. All eyes were trained on the night sky, trying to spot the aircraft scheduled to land any minute.

The pilot and the co-pilot for Air India flight 609, flying from Mumbai to Singapore with a stopover at the spanking new airport, had been handpicked for the inaugural flight. Cleared to land, the aircraft turned, aligned itself to the runway, and began its gradual descent.

The airport manager, Sharath Kumar, was the first to spot the lights of the aircraft. 'It's here!' he exclaimed excitedly.

'Where?' asked the VIPs surrounding him. They craned their necks and peered in the distance into the dark sky.

Lowering his binoculars, Sharath pointed toward a moving light, hardly visible to the naked eye. Everyone looked expectantly in the direction the airport manager was pointing. A few minutes passed, and then the approaching lights became clearly visible. The airplane hardly seemed to move at first, but then it began a slow descent towards the runway – it was a wonderful sight. There was loud applause. It was a proud moment for all who had toiled to turn a dream into reality.

In the cockpit, the captain stared at the runway and cursed angrily. 'Who the hell's that?' He had lowered his landing gear and was preparing to touch down when his eyes took in the surprising scene. Someone was standing on the runway, staring at the aircraft. Dressed in white, the figure was a stark contrast against the dark tarmac. 'Did you *see* that?' he asked the co-pilot.

'It's really careless of the authorities not to keep the runway clear. Should we inform the control tower?' replied the co-pilot.

Lit up brightly, the airport was still a few kilometres away. 'Contact the CT and report the matter. In the meantime, prepare to abort the landing.'

The co-pilot was reporting the situation to the CT when they saw the figure move away from the runway.

'Thank god she moved out in time!' The pilot wiped his brow and heaved a sigh of relief. *It's not a good beginning for the airport*, he thought.

The spectators watching the aircraft saw it falter ever so slightly, as though undecided about its course, but then the lights of the aircraft seemed to grow bigger and brighter as it glided gracefully towards the airport.

Just then, Sharath received a call from the CT. The pilot had reported seeing a woman on the runway. The captain was about to abort the landing when she hurried away, the manager was told. Sharath was furious. It was a serious error that could have caused many fatalities. He called the security officer, Pratap Sharma, and the chief of security, Agastya Roy, who were also looking after the entire construction activity. Taking them aside, he told them about the pilot's report.

'How could an unauthorized person possibly get onto the runway? I want this woman to be arrested, immediately,' barked the airport manager.

Orders were relayed, and within a couple of minutes, security personnel fanned out all over the area. They surrounded the runway, looking for the culprit. Meanwhile, the aircraft touched down amidst loud cheering. Other than the airport manager, Agastya, no one knew the reason why the aircraft had seemed to falter for a moment.

While the crowd gave the passengers a rousing reception, the security staff was busy trying to find the woman who had strayed onto the runway. After midnight, when the flight departed for Singapore, all the relevant CCTV camera footage was viewed, and everyone on duty questioned. But the security personnel drew a blank. Agastya could not fathom the reason for the unusual occurrence. He had taken all possible steps to ensure optimal security, but there was no doubt that the incident was a major lapse. It must have been some construction worker, he concluded.

Pratap carried out a thorough inspection of the runway and the area around it. There was no trace of anyone around, and he was baffled.

'I hope you have found the culprit,' Agastya said as soon as Pratap entered his office the next morning.

'We have scanned the area inch by inch. There was no one. It's impossible for anyone to disappear within the few minutes it took us to react. Either the pilot made a mistake or something spooky is going on.'

'We can't get away by claiming the pilot made an error. Both the pilot and co-pilot saw the woman, and they are amongst the best pilots in the fleet. Don't even mention the word spooky. No one's going to believe such a thing. There *must* be a logical explanation.'

'You won't believe this, but several guards have reported funny sightings during my interviews.'

'They must be drunk.'

'All of them can't be drunk, Agastya. I believe them. There's something spooky about this incident.'

'We'll have to do better than that, Pratap. I don't think the airport manager will buy your story.'

'I have investigated the matter, and I can assure you there was no security lapse.'

The two of them were discussing the details when Sharath called. 'Have you found the culprit?' he asked.

'We are still investigating,' Agastya replied. 'Security was unable to find anyone. The offender seems to have vanished within seconds.

'How is it possible for a woman to vanish?' Sharath thundered. His neck was in the noose, and he had no patience for nonsense. 'This is serious – someone has been negligent.'

'But ...'

'There's no time for ifs and buts. Join me at the CT in half an hour,' ordered the airport manager.

Agastya had a good track record. Sharath had known him for many years and was confident about his efficiency and track record. That was the reason he had chosen to work with him on the project.

Sharath moved to Bengaluru in December 2007 to take charge of the new airport, which was still under construction. He had been handpicked by the airport authorities, and he was delighted because the move gave him an opportunity to get away from the politics that hounded the airport in Delhi. Besides, Bengaluru was his hometown and his family was happy to move to their favourite city. What he hadn't known was that the project was riddled with problems and the progress would be painstakingly slow. He had been chosen to handle the venture because the predecessor had failed to deliver results, and time was at a premium. The bosses expected him to strictly adhere to the deadline for the completion of the airport.

Within a fortnight of reaching the city, Sharath realized he had made a mistake by accepting the job. But backing out would leave a blot on his brilliant career. He spent many a sleepless night trying to figure out his next move. And then he called Agastya.

The two of them had worked together at the Indira Gandhi International Airport in New Delhi while it was undergoing renovation. Agastya worked for a Singapore-based company that specialized in airport construction. He had vast experience in the field and could resolve all kinds of issues. The easy-going man was good at liaison work too. He had done a good job in Delhi, and the two of them got along very well. Sharath knew he could depend on the man. When he had proposed that Agastya work on the project in Bengaluru, he had jumped at the offer.

'I will be there as soon as I can,' Agastya promised.

A couple of days later, Sharath drove to the old airport to receive his friend. They hugged each other as Sharath said, 'I am so happy to see you here!' throwing a warm smile at Agastya.

'So am I! I never thought we would work together again.'

'You must be exhausted. I will drop you home now, and you can send for the car whenever you are ready to see the new airport. It's far from complete, of course.'

'Let's go to the construction site right away. The driver can drop me home later.' As the car changed lanes and raced towards the new airport, Agastya glanced out of the window. 'There's something about Bangalore that sets it apart from the other cities – I like it,' he said.

'Bangalore is a good place, all right,' Sharath agreed. 'The project, however, isn't going so well.'

'I can detect a note of regret in your tone. Aren't you happy to be here?'

'Perhaps.'

'Oh, come on, you couldn't have asked for a better position and prospects?'

'The place is wonderful. I have no complaints about that.'

'So what's the problem?'

'It's the project. The last few weeks have been quite terrible. There are too many hurdles to be crossed before we can make any progress. At the same time, the authorities are eager to inaugurate the airport.'

'Since when have you begun getting upset about hurdles? Don't worry, we'll handle it,' Agastya said, patting his friend's arm.

'That's why I wanted you here. With you working with me, I could get the airport going.'

They had reached the new airport and driven to the control tower, which offered a beautiful bird's-eye view of the area that stretched before their eyes.

'It's an impressive place,' said Agastya. He looked around the control tower. The furniture was in place, and the equipment had arrived and been laid out, but it would be a few months before the tower would be operational.

After they finished with the control tower, Sharath took Agastya on a tour of the entire area. He gave a detailed brief on the layout and the agencies at work. Having Agastya working with him, Sharath felt calmer and more confident. He shared the fears and the problems he faced. Many of the agencies involved in the project were not able to deliver results. Politics had crept in, delaying things. There were other problems too—thefts, pilfering, accidents, deaths, and security lapses. Sharath bared his soul to his friend, and Agastya gave him a patient hearing, saying nothing till Sharath finished. The two cups of tea that lay on the table had gone cold.

'There have been unusual delays, and things are slowly getting out of hand. There's pressure on us to get things ready by 30 March 2008 for the inauguration.'

'But it's the end of December already,' protested Agastya. 'There's so much to be done before the inauguration.'

'I agree – we can't get the airport ready in three months.'

'Do you think we should ask for an extension?' Sharath asked.

'I can't say till I have gone through everything in detail.'

'Take your time. Settle down, and then we will discuss everything.'

But Agastya went to work sooner than expected. He made several rounds of the airport along with his deputy, Pratap. The two of them worked through many nights, poring over notes and updates on the airport. Sharath would often join in their discussions. In the end, they decided it would be best for Sharath to ask for an extension. The inauguration would have to be delayed. While several things were under their control, it was not possible to hasten the air traffic control services as the agencies involved did not answer to them.

After much effort and many presentations, Sharath got the inauguration date shifted to 11 May. They now had forty extra days to finish the project and put activities into high gear. Everyone was performing beyond their duty. Agastya managed to get funds released and appointed additional labour, and raw material arrived without delay. While Agastya did the liaison and paperwork, Pratap supervised the construction. They wanted to leave nothing to chance, so they often slept on the airport premises. The heightened activity had some ill effects too. Some ghastly accidents took place.

Agastya worked late every night. He went through all the standard operating procedures and revised them wherever required. He visited the security control room to check the placement and effectiveness of the CCTVs, spoke to the people who manned the set-up, and was on his toes through the day. He had an excellent reputation and wanted to live up to it.

Despite the accidents and hiccups, things moved efficiently, and all was set for the inauguration on 11 May. Unfortunately, it had to be delayed again. This time, it was because of reasons beyond their control. Some politicians wanted their names to be printed on the invitation card, and so the cards had to be reprinted. The new invitation cards, with sixty names, turned out to be six pages long. A fresh inauguration date was announced. The airport would now open on 24 May.

Sharath, Agastya and Pratap finally got things moving, and the inauguration went off without a hitch. Everything was going well until the sighting of the strange woman on the runway during the inaugural flight.

Things were in a tizzy for a couple of days. The new airport was a busy place, with dozens of international flights departing and arriving every few hours. With so many things happening at the airport, they put the incident on the back burner.

A couple of days later, Pratap was passing through the arrival lounge at night when he noticed a commotion. A dazed-looking young man was being led away by a CISF guard. Several curious passengers stopped by next to them.

The crowd parted as Pratap approached the man. 'What's the matter?' he asked the guard. 'Is he ill?'

'He's in shock, sir.'

'Call the doctor,' he told the guard, who sprinted away to carry out the order.

'Please don't bother, I'll be alright,' said the man as he took a sip of the water offered by a co-passenger.

'We can't allow you to leave until the doctor examines you.' Pratap looked doubtfully at the man, who appeared shaken.

'I was on the same flight as him,' said the man's co-passenger. 'It seems a woman knocked on the window near his seat just as the aircraft touched down. She was *outside*.'

'Did you have too much to drink?' Pratap had dealt with several passengers who drank too much alcohol on international flights. Either they misbehaved or were unruly.

'I didn't have any alcohol!' the young man protested.

'It's not only him. He had a window seat, so he saw her clearly. In fact, the passenger in the next seat also saw the woman outside the window. She was dressed in white and knocked frantically on the window,' the woman said. 'He was so shaken that he called the flight attendant. She couldn't come since she had returned to her seat for landing.'

'You can check with the crew if you don't believe me.'

It must be a joke, Pratap thought. The guy must be crazy. It was just not possible for someone to knock on the window of the aircraft from the outside while the aircraft was landing. Since he was too busy to spare time for a delusional passenger, Pratap dropped the matter. In the meantime, the passenger left the lounge after the doctor declared him fit to leave.

'What was the commotion about?' Agastya asked Pratap when he heard about the incident the next morning. The two of them were walking to the cargo village, where a building was under construction. 'First the pilot and co-pilot spotted a woman on the runway, and now she's knocking on windows.'

'I think the guy was delusional. What he's saying can't be possible.'

Although the matter was dropped, weird incidents continued to be reported by the passengers and the ground staff. These were serious incidents that couldn't be ignored, so Pratap started to investigate. He began compiling a list of the unusual incidents which had been brought to his notice. Once he had gathered the details of a few incidents, Pratap prepared a PowerPoint presentation. He requested Agastya to spare an hour so that he could brief him about the matter.

'Why don't you come to my office?' Agastya responded. 'I am curious to know the details.'

A few minutes later, Pratap began the presentation. The first slide was captioned 'The Mysterious Thefts at the Cargo Village'.

For a long time, equipment meant for the airport was being stolen from the storehouse in the cargo village. They vanished at regular intervals during the night. The windows were bolted from inside, and the door of each room sealed every night, but the pilferage did not stop. The storekeeper noticed that the packages were missing when he opened the storehouse in the morning. No one could find out how and where the packages vanished.

Night guards reported seeing a ghost walking near the store at night. Pratap ordered that CCTV cameras be placed at the store entrance, but that did not help – the packages still went missing. Finally, along with a guard, he locked himself in the storehouse one night.

At around midnight, he noticed that a window on the first floor flew open. A cable was cast from the storehouse to a truck parked on the road across the perimeter wall. The thief used a pulley and steel cable to pick up the packages and convey them to the truck. Once the packages had been transferred to the truck, the cable was pulled up and the window closed. The storekeeper turned out to be an accomplice of the thief, and they were handed over to the police, and the mystery of the thefts was solved.

The next slide was about the strange sightings.

'A couple of days ago, the night guard reported seeing a woman on the terrace of the main building of the cargo village at night. He wondered how she had entered the building, which had been locked and sealed. At first, the senior officer dismissed his report, thinking he had been drunk on duty. Later, on his insistence, a few more guards were put on duty. Once again, a guard spotted the lady on the terrace. A few minutes later, another guard found her roaming in room number four on the ground floor. Both the guards submitted their reports, and a thorough search was carried out. Surprisingly, the seal on the door of room number four was intact.'

'Did you check the CCTVs?' Agastya interrupted the presentation.

'I did, the next day. I also placed additional CCTV cameras to monitor the entire building.'

'Were you able to catch the culprit?'

'No, we couldn't. She was seen again after three days. We were surprised that the CCTVs had failed to capture her. There was nothing except some moving orbs of light.'

'Hmmm. Is there any possibility of the guards being drunk?'

'Nope! We ensured they were not drunk, and I placed them in pairs.'

There was silence for a few minutes and then Agastya asked, 'Has anyone seen her again?'

'Yes, two guards spotted the woman last night. The series of incidents set me thinking, and I began investigating. I discovered that a woman working as a labourer in the cargo wing had met with an accident a few months back. An iron girder had fallen on her and she died,' Pratap said, continuing with his next slide.

'When did the accident take place?'

'It was soon after Sharath took charge. He was under pressure to complete the project, and he asked the contractors to speed things up. It was during that time that a few accidents took place.'

He pressed a key, and the next slide showed up on the screen. It was about the runway accident.

'This happened a day before the inauguration. I was catching up with some paperwork in my office,' said Pratap. 'Suddenly,

I saw two cars racing down the runway at breakneck speed. One of them knocked down a labourer who was crossing the runway. The woman died. Although the contractor hushed up the matter by paying the family, the resentment continued to boil for a while.'

There was a pause and then Agastya asked, 'Are you implying that the woman who roams around the cargo area is a ghost?'

'I am convinced it is a ghost. Remember the sudden appearance in front of the inaugural flight, and then the passenger reporting that he saw a woman knocking on the window of the aircraft?'

'It's *unbelievable*,' Agastya mumbled. He didn't believe in ghosts.

The next slide was about an incident that took place on a conveyer belt in the arrival area. It had taken place a few days before the inauguration. The conveyer belt had been stationary, and a sweeper, who had been cleaning the arrival lounge, sat down on the conveyer belt for a quick rest. Suddenly, the belt began to move because the electricians testing the belts switched them on. The sweeper was taken by surprise and lost her balance. She fell headfirst and died on the spot.'

Agastya gasped. Pratap pressed a key, and the next slide appeared. It had a strange title – 'Crying Baby'.

'The conveyer belt began making strange squeaking sounds a couple of days after the accident. A mechanic was summoned, and he repaired it. It worked smoothly for a few hours and then started squeaking again. It sounded like a baby crying. No matter how many times it was repaired, the crying sounds didn't stop.'

'Come to think of it, I also heard that sound. Has it not been repaired?'

'No. We just can't repair the belt and get rid of that sound.'

Agastya asked, 'Is it the same belt the sweeper fell from?'

'That's right. The post-mortem report stated that the woman was pregnant at the time of her death.' Pratap shook his head sadly.

'It's all so depressing. Are there many such cases?'

'There are five more. All of them spooky in nature.'

'Let's inform Sharath. I'll ask him to come here.'

Pratap ran through the entire presentation again once Sharath joined them. As expected, the airport manager was aghast at the number of unexplained occurrences. 'These are truly spooky,' he commented with a worried frown. 'I wonder if there are any remedies for this problem,' asked Sharath, looking at the two men. They had no answer. 'Please don't share these details with anyone. Let's keep it between the three of us.' He stood up and sighed. Not in his wildest dreams had he imagined that the spanking new airport was inhabited by ghosts.'

The gaunt man, finishing his story, added, 'To tell the truth, my friend Sharath has experienced several spooky incidents in his life. I wish he was here to tell you some of those hair-raising experiences.'

'Incredible!' commented the anthropologist.

4

THE GHOST WITH A SWEET TOOTH

Uday was too exhausted and sleepy to listen to any more stories. The fact that he didn't believe in ghosts made it doubly taxing for him to continue sitting at the dining table, but Keshavmama showed no inclination to stop the storytelling session.

'Well, does anyone else have an interesting story?' asked Keshavmama. Turning to his nephew, who was getting restless, he said, 'You can't leave the table during a session. Wait till everyone has finished.'

Keshavmama looked expectantly at his guests gathered around the table. He sounded disappointed and said, 'Shall we assume that there are no more stories, and the party is over?'

'I have an interesting story,' exclaimed a lady seated on the far side of the table. Dressed in a black sari, she was wearing a lot of jewellery. 'It's a rather funny one actually.'

'Hear, hear!' the portly fellow thumped the table enthusiastically. 'I love funny stories. Do share it with us.'

So, the lady began narrating her tale, and Uday was forced to listen to yet another story.

'Arjun, a hyperactive ten-year-old boy, and the only son of Mr and Mrs Murthy, was feeling restless. The lockdown caused by the coronavirus disease had been tough on everybody, but it was worse for children. Forced to stay indoors, they were raring to go out and play with friends. 'Peering into a computer screen or playing indoor games is no fun!' Arjun had declared as soon as the lockdown was imposed. What had appeared to be a short-term imprisonment now seemed to be slated to last a long time. There was no sign of the lockdown being lifted, and he felt suffocated inside the house.

Although he was busy with online classes, the spare hours were a cause of concern. The boy had never been a fan of television, had no love for reading anything other than comic books, and computer games failed to excite him. Two months was a long time, and Arjun's parents were at their wits' end. They were both working from home and wanted no disturbance. The household help was not allowed to enter the posh colony, and they had to do their own chores. The boy's whining added to their woes, but they didn't know how to keep their son engaged.

One morning, while his parents were busy with office work, Arjun stole out of the house to meet his classmate near the gate of the playing ground. The two boys were thrilled with the prospect of playing together. Their escapade came to an abrupt end when the watchman shouted at them to return home, threatening to call the police if they didn't do so immediately. His cricket bat and ball in hand, Arjun returned home, unhappy with the state of affairs. His troubles, however, had not ended. His mother, who had just taken a coffee break, had discovered his absence. She called out to her husband and they began searching for their errant son. They had just called the security when Arjun returned home. Fireworks followed. His mother lamented and cried, while his father punished him with one tight slap.

It was evening, but the boy remained locked in his room, refusing to join his parents for tea.

'You shouldn't have reprimanded him,' Mrs Murthy rebuked her husband.

'That boy is totally lacking in discipline,' fumed Mr Murthy. 'You have spoiled him with all your cosseting and pampering. Ticking him off sometimes will help him become a better person.'

'That's what you think!' Mrs Murthy snorted.

'There is no need to call him. Missing tea won't make any difference to him. In fact, don't call him for dinner – it may make him repentant.'

Mrs Murthy waited for her son to emerge from his room, but Arjun stayed in. Worried, she knocked on his door and entered the room. Her son was lying on the bed.

'Get up, Aru. Come and have tea. Your father and I are disappointed by your behaviour, but we can talk about that later.' She walked up to the bed and shook her son.

Arjun's body was burning up with fever. Alarmed, she called out to her husband. The thermometer showed that the boy had a high fever. The worried couple called Dr Raman, who prescribed some medicines. Despite all the medicines, two days later, the fever refused to come down. He lost his appetite and refused to eat.

The next morning, the frantic Mrs Murthy called the doctor again. 'Arjun's fever hasn't subsided,' she cried. 'He refuses to eat and has a severe headache. Do you think he's got COVID?'

'Although I haven't come across any cases of coronavirus in children. It would be good to get him tested, though. Why don't you take him to Victoria Hospital? I will put in a word with my friend, Dr Shankar, who is a senior surgeon at the hospital,' said Dr Raman.

A few minutes later, the Murthy family set out for the hospital, and Arjun was soon subjected to the COVID-19 test. Since they were at the hospital, the Murthys took the test, too. The next day, the result confirmed that Arjun was not suffering from coronavirus, but the couple tested positive for the virus. The child had contracted chicken pox.

'Can you keep your son with a friend or relative for two weeks?' asked Dr Shankar. 'Since the two of you have tested positive, it is necessary to keep Arjun away from you.'

Mrs Murthy thought for a while but did not have a solution. The couple had a few relatives in Bangalore, but it would not be right to keep a boisterous boy like Arjun with them. Her uncle and aunt were aged and ailing. Her husband's parents stayed too far away. Besides, with no friends or distractions, Arjun would be bored and drive them crazy. As for friends, she was hesitant to ask them to house her son for more than a couple of days.

Dr Shankar realized her dilemma. 'We can keep him at the hospital,' he suggested. 'The child can be admitted here till the two of you recover.'

Mrs Murthy had never stayed away from her son and was reluctant to let him stay in the hospital. It was only after much persuasion from her husband that she relented. But as soon as he heard, Arjun threw a tantrum. Being imprisoned at home was bad enough, but the hospital was the worst punishment he could imagine. It took a lot of coaxing and bribing to make him agree. Arjun had been asking his parents for an e-reader to read his favourite comic books for a long time. It was only after Mr Murthy promised to get him one that he calmed down.

The hospital was a depressing place for the energetic boy. He found himself restricted to a small room across a common ward and could hear some of the patients groaning through the day and night, and it only made him more irritable. No one seemed to be interested in befriending the lonely boy. He missed his mother's cooking and threw tantrums and refused to have his medicines and meals. His body was covered with itchy rashes, which were fast turning into blisters. They made him crankier than ever.

He hated the hospital, especially the strict matron who came on her rounds twice a day. She scolded him for being a fussy boy. The other nurses were kind but too busy to devote much time to him. Arjun waited for a visit from his parents, but they were in quarantine.

After receiving several complaints about his unruly behaviour, Dr Shankar came to visit Arjun. 'What is it you want, my boy?' he asked.

'I want to go home,' Arjun replied.

'That's not possible. You are not well, and your parents are not in the right condition to look after you.'

'I want an e-reader!'

'Will that make you feel better?'

'I think so,' Arjun nodded.

'I will speak to your parents, and I am sure they will send you one,' said the doctor. 'Do you promise to listen to the nurses now?'

The very next day, Arjun's parents sent a tablet with Dr Raman, and the boy was overjoyed. He spent his time reading books on his newly acquired gadget. There was not much he could do since he was confined to bed. Starting with Enid Blyton and her Famous Five series, he read the Secret Seven and then graduated to the Harry Potter series. When he was bored with reading, he played games on the tablet.

Of all the things, Arjun missed home food the most. The bland food supplied by the hospital killed the little appetite his sickness allowed. He often left his tray untouched. When he was hungry, he dug into the reserve of chocolates his parents had left, but the stock was depleting fast, and something would have to be done. He soon threw a tantrum, demanding food from home. The nurses had noticed the untouched tray by the boy's bedside, and it had worried them. They didn't know about the chocolates, of course. Would the boy starve himself to death? They reported the matter to the doctors, who called the Murthys.

Mrs Murthy was agitated. She demanded that her husband deliver home-cooked food to Arjun.

'How's that possible? I am in quarantine!'

'I don't care. My son is starving – you will have to find a way.'

'Your son is a spoiled brat. He's resorting to arm-twisting to get his way. Everyone's eating hospital food, but only your precious son has problems with it.'

'Well, if you don't do something about the matter, I will deliver the food myself.'

'Let me speak to Dr Shankar,' Mr Murthy said, throwing up his hands in surrender. 'He may have a solution.'

As expected, Dr Shankar came up with a brilliant idea. 'Hari, a ward boy who works here, lives close to your residence. I am sure he'll bring the food for a small fee.'

And so, they arranged for a tiffin carrier to be delivered to the hospital. Mrs Murthy would prepare Arjun's favourite dishes, load the food into the carrier and leave it outside the door. Hari would pick it up, sanitize it and deliver it to the boy. He would bring the carrier back the next morning and pick up another one with food. It was an arrangement that satisfied everyone. Arjun relished home food, Hari made extra money, and Mrs Murthy was happy.

Mrs Murthy, who never forgot to send some sweets along with the food, sent a note with the tiffin every day. She always wanted to know if Arjun wanted anything special the next day. The nurses heaved a sigh of relief. Occupied with his tablet, and satisfied with home food, Arjun threw tantrums less frequently.

A week passed, and Arjun was happy with his tablet, home food, lots of sweets, and a new friend. Revathi, a junior nurse, was on the night shift. She loved reading too. The best part was that she liked the bratty boy, and the two discussed the books he read. She often borrowed the tablet when Arjun went to sleep. In return, she brought him chocolates.

Sometimes, when the story was engrossing, Arjun continued to read in the dim night light, much after they had switched the main lights off. Revathi, who did the rounds at night, would often find the boy reading.

In the meantime, the Murthys were retested for COVID-19. This time, they tested negative and were no longer required to remain in quarantine. The first thing they did was to visit the hospital and hand over Arjun's favourite food to a nurse. The boy had almost recovered. His scabs were falling off, and he was feeling much better. But Dr Shankar wanted to play it safe by keeping him for a few more days.

This did not please the boy, who was impatient to go home.

'Please, Arjun,' his mother pleaded. 'You have been a brave boy for so long – just a couple of more days, and then we'll take you home,' she said, offering him some Mysore pak, his favourite sweet.

Arjun turned his face away and refused to eat the sweets, so she left them by the bedside.

The Murthys could not visit him the next morning, and Mrs Murthy sent him food and sweets through the ward boy.

It surprised her to see Arjun in a foul mood when she visited him in the evening.

'Why did you take away the Mysore pak? I wanted to eat it after dinner, but it wasn't there,' he complained.

It perplexed his mother. She remembered having placed the sweet by his bedside. 'I left it here, Aru.' She pointed.

'No, it wasn't there!' Arjun insisted. Nothing she said could soothe the irritated boy.

Finally, Mr Murthy went out and bought some Mysore pak.

'I wonder what happened to the pak I left by Aru's bedside?' said his wife as they drove home.

'You may have carried it back by mistake,' said her husband.

'Impossible! Arjun is very fond of eating some after a meal.'

'It can happen, Mala. Just put a few extra pieces the next time.'

Mrs Murthy felt guilty. Had she really forgotten? The next day, she opened the tiffin carrier at the hospital and showed the sweets to her son. 'Here are some extra pieces to make up for yesterday.'

That perked up the boy, and he smiled.

'You haven't had your dinner, Arjun,' Revathi said later that evening, pointing to the tiffin carrier that lay next to a clean plate on the bedside table. 'It's past 10 p.m., and the lights will be switched off now. Finish your dinner and go to bed.'

Arjun, who had been reading a mystery story, had not realized how much time had passed. He opened the tiffin carrier and found the sweets missing again. How was that possible? His mother had shown him the sweets. *It must be Revathi. She must have taken the sweets away when I was not looking. She could have asked for them. I wouldn't have refused. There were too many of them – I couldn't have finished the entire lot.*

He didn't want to complain about the stolen sweets. Revathi was kind to him, and Arjun didn't want to create any trouble for her. He decided to count the number of sweets in the tiffin carrier at night the next day. To his surprise, the sweets vanished once again. The amount of food was decreasing too. He asked his mother to pack extra food for him. That failed to work. The sweets and food disappeared again.

Arjun was now angry. *Revathi is a greedy woman. There were enough sweets, but she didn't leave a single one for me.* But it was so unlike her. The thief had to be someone else. He decided to be watchful so that he could catch the culprit.

'I think it's a ghost,' Arjun declared when his mother visited. 'Last night, I ate early. But I left a few sweets and pretended to be asleep. Actually, I kept a watch so that I could catch the culprit.'

Mrs Murthy was amused. 'So, did you?'

'That's the strangest part! I couldn't see anyone, but I heard the sound of chomping and the sweets disappeared. It's a ghost. The more I think about it, the more I am convinced that it is.'

'You have been reading too many stories, I think,' his mother ruffled his hair affectionately. 'Did you read a ghost story last night?'

'No, but I am sure a ghost is stealing my food.'

'Aru! Don't think of ghosts before going to bed – they'll only give you bad dreams,' she warned her son, but her mind was in a whirl. Her son had a vivid imagination, but he wouldn't conjure up ghosts eating his food. Ghost or no ghost, someone had taken his food.

Mrs Murthy was not one to take things lightly. Not only was her son missing his sweets, but he had also now begun talking about ghosts. She decided to complain to the authorities. It was a holiday, and she couldn't find any senior doctors around. She took her complaint to a young duty medical officer, who was on his rounds.

'It must be a rat,' he said, brushing off her complaint with a laugh.

Not convinced with his explanation, Mrs Murthy waylaid a nurse. 'Are there rats in the ward?' she asked the nurse.

The question startled the nurse, who was terrified of rats. But she had seen none in the ward.

It must be the nurse on night duty. Mrs Murthy was convinced – *I must complain to the authorities*.

She called the hospital superintendent, Dr Krishnamurthy, and narrated the story of the vanishing food and sweets.

'May I request you to meet me when you come here this evening,' he said. The superintendent was an efficient man who had worked at the Victoria Hospital for many years. He knew every little detail about the hospital.

That evening, Mrs Murthy was on the warpath. She entered his office and poured out her anger. 'I am surprised that such a prestigious hospital has rats running all over the place ...' she waved her hands to emphasize the words. 'Either the rats or the staff, someone has been stealing the food from my son's carrier. I will not ...'

Dr Krishnaswamy raised his hand to silence the woman. 'I understand your feelings, Mrs Murthy. Will you give me a moment please and listen to what I have to say?' He pressed a buzzer and asked for two cups of tea.

'That won't be necessary,' said Mrs Murthy edgily. 'I know you are busy, and I don't want to take much of your time,' she said, fidgeting impatiently in her seat.

'I think you will need it,' the superintendent smiled. 'Your complaint doesn't surprise me, Mrs Murthy. Such things have been happening here for several years. Please bear with me, and I will tell you everything. However, I will request you to keep the information confidential. We don't want to upset our patients.'

A serving staff came in with two cups of steaming tea and placed them on the table. Mrs Murthy sat back without looking at the cup, waiting for the superintendent to speak.

'The story goes back to 1944. Major Smith was posted here in Bangalore during the Second World War. This was when the Japanese Army, having made their way from Burma, entered Assam. The major was sent to Assam to beat back the attack, but his family continued to live here. It was a Sunday, and Major Smith's wife and son were going to the Trinity Church for mass when they met with an accident. The son suffered multiple fractures and was hospitalized here, staying about a month.'

'Dr Krishnaswamy, I am sure neither of us has the time for stories. This can wait for some other time. Let's address the matter at hand.'

'Patience, Mrs Murthy. Please let me finish first. I promise to answer all your queries.'

'This place was like a jungle at that time. Not just rats, snakes also wandered around this hospital. The hospital authorities employed some local snake catchers to get rid of snakes, but rats were another matter. Unfortunately, they couldn't find a Pied Piper. and the rats became a menace.

'Dr Richardson was the head of this hospital back then. He was a close friend of Major Smith's, and Mrs Smith requested him to take special care of Peter, their son, while he was here. "Please keep the rats away from his food," she begged. "I don't want him to get some disease."

'But the rats were a smart lot. They had learned how to avoid the rat traps placed all around the hospital. Interestingly, they were not a discriminating lot. They treated all patients equally and nibbled at everyone's food.'

The story was interesting. Mrs Murthy straightened up in her seat.

'Like your son, Peter was very fond of sweets. His mother sent him cakes, pastries, and other desserts with every meal. The rats seemed to have a sweet tooth. They loved Peter's sweets and nibbled on them with delight. Worried about the boy's health, Richardson decided to do something about the rats. One night, after Peter ate his dinner and went to sleep, the doctor placed poison in the leftover food in the room.'

'Did the rats take the bait?'

'No! Not a single rat died,' Dr Krishnaswamy chuckled. 'But the next morning, Mariam, the nurse on night duty, was found dead. The post-mortem revealed that she had consumed the poisoned food.'

Mrs Murthy gasped. Was the superintendent indicating that Revathi had eaten Arjun's sweets?

'Can you see the link?'

'Yes, the nurse ...'

'Well, after Mariam's death, some patients discovered that their dinner had started to vanish. They reported that a lady in a nurse's uniform roamed the wards by night. A nurse on duty confirmed that she had seen Mariam while she was on her rounds, dressed in her white uniform. Night after night, patients saw the lady wandering around the hospital. Food, especially sweets, continued to disappear. No matter how strictly it was watched, food just vanished.'

Mrs Murthy picked up the cup of tea and took a sip.

'And then?'

'Finally, Mariam's mother consulted a witch doctor. He suggested that she place food in front of her daughter's photo at night. A plate of food, with Mariam's favourite sweets, was placed before her picture. By morning, it was all gone.'

'It worked?'

'Yes, it did. As long as Mariam's mother was alive, she continued to carry out the ritual of placing food in front of her daughter's picture, and our patients enjoyed their dinners with no problems thereafter.'

'Then why is this happening now? It's been happening for the last three days!'

'Now that Mariam's mother is no more, her son Kumar and his wife, place dinner in front of Mariam's photo. Unfortunately, Kumar had to undergo bypass surgery a few days ago, and his wife is looking after him in this hospital. There is no one to serve Mariam dinner, so she is haunting the hospital and eating the patients' food.'

'Isn't it too early for Kumar to undergo a heart surgery?'

'I think you forget that Mariam died in 1944. Her son was two years old at the time of her death. He is seventy-nine now. He is quite healthy and will soon recover, don't you worry. Kumar's wife has been requested to place dinner before Mariam's photo, so no more disappearing sweets from today.'

'It's an incredible story! Thank you, Doctor, for sparing your time.' Mrs Murthy walked out of his office, unable to believe the strange story.

That night, over dinner, she shared the story narrated by the superintendent with her husband.

'That guy must be nuts! He should have tried some other stunt to save his staff.' Mr Murthy laughed away the tale.

'It's unbelievable, all right,' she agreed.

True to the superintendent's words, Arjun's sweets no longer vanished because Kumar's wife had resumed placing food before Mariam's photograph.

The next day, the boy was discharged from the hospital, and his parents arrived to take him home. Someday, she would share the story with her son, Mrs Murthy decided.'

5

THE HAUNTED AIRCRAFT CARRIER

'That was truly funny!' said Keshavmama as voices began rising around the table.

'My turn now,' a reedy voice rang across the table.

Uday suppressed another yawn and shook his head sadly. At this rate, he was not likely to get any sleep. It seemed as though every person had a story to share.

The reedy voice started narrating his story with much enthusiasm.

'How could he behave in such an appalling manner? What if I didn't find my way back to the cabin?' Roshni raged as they climbed up the stairs for breakfast. Her eyes flashed with anger.

Her husband, Amar, was reluctant to take the bait.

'It's all right, Rosh,' he said, trying to soothe his irate wife. 'You found your way back, and that's all that matters.'

'It's not all right,' she continued as they entered the dining hall. 'This is an unknown place with so many passages – one could easily get lost! To be honest, I was quite frightened. Let's face it, Amar, the guy behaved irresponsibly. He has no business being employed on a ship this size. We should complain.'

The lavish buffet in the dining hall did nothing to improve Roshni's mood. Despite Amar's reluctance to follow up on the matter, she continued to insist that they lodge a written complaint against the person who abandoned her in the dark passage.

'I was so disturbed that I could not sleep the entire night. Don't you think that matters? We paid through the nose to spend a night on this ship – the least I deserve is a good night's sleep.'

Not one to miss an opportunity to enjoy excellent food, Amar turned a deaf ear to her ranting. The thing was over and done with. There was no reason to go on about what had happened the previous night. They were not likely to return to the ship ever.

The previous night, Roshni had wanted to go to the washroom after dinner in the dining hall. After finding both the washrooms occupied, she had wandered around looking for another one and had lost her way. A staff member, who was passing by, had helpfully offered to assist her.

'There's a washroom at the end of the passage, I will lead you there,' the charming young man had remarked as he led her down the passage. His nameplate had identified him as Allen Smith. 'I hope you are enjoying your stay on the ship.'

'It's quite an impressive ship, and the arrangements are excellent. To be honest, I have never been inside such a massive ship!' Roshni had said, hastening to keep pace with him. The surrounding temperature had dropped suddenly, and she had wrapped her coat around her tightly. 'I would be quite lost if I were left on my own,' she admitted.

'That's true. Navigating through the different areas can prove quite challenging if one is not used to the ship. There's a maze of passages that lead to different places, and one doesn't know which one to take.'

Allen had continued to chat in a friendly manner as they went up a flight of steps and walked along yet another passage. By now, Roshni had lost her bearing and blindly followed the young man. He had turned along the bend, and when she had rounded the corner, Allen had disappeared. Surprised, she had looked around. The passage had been narrow, and there was no place to hide. But the chap seemed to have vanished into the thin air.

'Allen?' her frightened voice had carried through the passage. Her hands grew clammy with anxiety, and she shivered. Fear gripped her in its icy talons. Where was the man?

Crying and stumbling through the narrow passages, Roshni had rushed forward, chased by terrifying shadows. There had not been a soul in sight, and she had realized she was lost. Cold and frightened, she had stumbled along the passages, and it was a long time before she found her way back to the cabin.

'Where were you?' Amar had stared at his wife's ashen face with concern. She was trembling.

Roshni had broken into loud sobs and clung to her husband, who had just stepped out of the cabin to look for her. 'He ... he ... disappeared so suddenly. I ... I ... was lost.'

'Who? I am confused.'

'That man ... he.' Roshni fumbled for the right words.

Amar was perplexed at her nervousness, he tried to pacify his wife. 'I waited in the dining hall for a long time. When you didn't return, I thought you'd come back to the cabin. In fact, I was getting ready to search for you.' He had stroked her hair and led her to the bed. 'Do you want coffee?' he asked.

'No, don't leave me alone. I am so scared.'

Lovingly, he had tucked her into the bed and continued to stroke her head. 'It's all right, don't cry.'

It had taken a long time for her to fall into a restless sleep, but she didn't let go of Amar's hand.

The newly married couple was on a trip to the US at Amar's elder brother Avinash's invitation. His hectic schedule had prevented Avinash from attending Amar's wedding. He had sent them a pair of return tickets, along with the assurance of a good time. Looking forward to a fortnight of fun and enjoyment, the couple landed at the San Jose International Airport on a cold morning. It was their first trip to the US.

'I have taken a couple of days off to show you around,' Avinash had informed his brother as he drove them to the luxurious apartment where he lived with his wife Aparna and their five-year-old son, Vicky.'

'You better atone for your absence at my wedding,' Amar had warned. 'I won't make it easy for you.'

'Don't you worry. The two of you won't have a dull moment. Aparna has made an elaborate itinerary for your visit.'

On the very first weekend, Avinash had taken them on a day trip to the Golden Gate Bridge. It had been a hectic day as they went around the San Francisco Bay and saw the adjoining areas. Roshni had been spellbound by the bridge, but Amar's fascination lay in the *USS Hornet*, a Second World War aircraft carrier that had been converted into a museum.

'It's so impressive!' he had exclaimed as they watched it from a distance.

'Would you like to go up on the ship? They have different kinds of tours around the ship. I would recommend the "History, Mystery" overnight experience. You will sleep where the crew slept and get an opportunity to explore around from 6 p.m. to 9 a.m. the next morning. Do you want me to book tickets?' Avinash had asked.

The offer had been too tempting to refuse.

'It would be nice if you joined us with Aparna and Vicky,' said Amar.

'That'll not be possible because the tour is meant for individuals above the age of sixteen, and we can't leave Vicky alone. In any case, Aparna and I have already spent a night on the ship on our honeymoon. The funny incidents that took place during that night make for an interesting story. I will tell you the story after you return. So, should I book the tickets?'

The couple had exchanged a look and nodded happily. For Roshni, who worked as a reporter for a newspaper, it provided an opportunity to write an interesting story when she returned to India. What the two brothers hadn't told her was that the

USS Hornet was rumoured to be haunted by the spirits of the 200 sailors who had died onboard.

A couple of days later, with their tickets booked, the two of them had made their way to the ship. There had been many guidelines to be adhered to, like wearing comfortable clothes and closed-toe walking shoes, luggage size restrictions, and type of cameras to be taken with mandatory neck straps and torches. There also been warnings about steep ladders, cold compartments and a host of other things.

Twenty guests had boarded the ship with Roshni and Amar. Everyone was looking forward to spending an exciting night onboard. What was most thrilling was that its docents were veterans who had earlier served on ships and aircraft carriers like the *USS Hornet*.

The visitors had been welcomed by Stephen Douglas, an old naval guy who had served on an aircraft carrier for many years before he retired. He had rattled off a list of dos and don'ts as they stood on the deck. The most important, he had said, was the need to stick around together. 'There have been eight ships named the *USS Hornet*, the first of them having been commissioned in 1775. This one, also known as the *USS Hornet* (CV-12), is the last one in the series. It is 250 meters long, and 35 meters wide. During its heyday, about 1,350 men of the navy and 850 from the air force made up the crew of this ship,' Stephen had told them. 'It could attain a speed of about 60 km per hour and carry over 100 aircraft on it. Hornet's combat strength lay in its aircraft. The highly trained pilots and aircrews and the specialized aircraft that operated from her flight deck proved their worth during World War II.'

The guests had all been amazed at the size of the ship. The enormous guns protruding from different parts of the ship in different directions made it look like an iron fortress, and the deck was huge and flat, just like a runway. It was under this runway that the history and mystery of the aircraft carrier lay.

'Though this carrier was supposed to be called Kearsarge, it was given the name *USS Hornet* after the previous *USS Hornet* (CV-8), a huge aircraft carrier, was sunk in the Battle of Santa Cruz by the Japanese on 26 October 1942,' their guide had droned as he led them into the Officers' Stateroom.

They had traipsed around the elegantly equipped admiral's and captain's cabins and walked along the hangar bays, radio centre, flight control rooms, engine rooms, galleys, tailor shop, laundry rooms, and various other rooms.

Roshni had clicked dozens of pictures and made a note of the information so that she could write a story for the newspaper.

'The *USS Hornet* (CV-12) was launched on 30 August 1943. The crew called it *The Grey Ghost*,' the guide had continued his narration. 'It saw action all over the world and took part in the Korean War, Vietnam War, and was involved in the recovery of Apollo 11 astronauts from the Pacific Ocean on their return from the moon in 1969. It was decommissioned in 1970 after about thirty-seven years of service. In 1998, it was thrown open to the public as the *USS Hornet* – Sea, Air, and Space Museum in its present location.'

It had been an extensive tour and a tiring evening with dozens of exciting things to see and absorb. The dinner that followed had been very satisfying, and Amar was quite happy with his experience, but Roshni was in no mood to relent. The fiasco of the previous night had left an unpleasant taste in her mouth. She refused to enjoy breakfast and continued to harp on the nasty experience.

'All right, we will make a complaint,' Amar finally yielded. 'First, let's finish breakfast.'

Soon, more people arrived for breakfast, and the tables were buzzing with conversation. A group of guests pulled up chairs to share a table. They discussed their experiences on the ship.

Roshni overheard a lady complaining, 'Someone kept switching the lights on and off throughout the night. It was so annoying. At first, I suspected someone was trying to play a prank, but when I got up to investigate, I found no one around.'

'It's a prank all right. It isn't the humans playing the fool,' chuckled her husband, who had visited the ship earlier. 'There are ghosts on this ship.'

Soon, there was a babble of voices as a couple of other guests shared their experiences. 'That's quite true. I heard someone knocking on the door of our cabin. I got up to check but found no one,' said another woman.

Darting a knowing look at her husband, Roshni got up and joined the guests at the adjoining table.

'I had a weird experience last night,' she told the guests. 'A guy called Allen Smith offered to help me find the washroom. He suddenly disappeared, leading me into a passage, and I lost my way. It was a creepy experience. I don't know if it was a ghost or a human, but I intend to find out.'

'It must be a ghost, my dear,' said an elderly lady. 'The ship is said to be haunted, and we are on a paranormal tour. It's the spirits of all those dead sailors, you see. Hundreds of people have died onboard, and there are likely to be some paranormal activities. In fact, I woke up around midnight and felt the bed rocking as if we were sailing.'

Was the ship really haunted? The reporter in her was aroused. She wanted to write about the paranormal happenings on board the ship. It would make an interesting story.

The other women around the table nodded as Amar joined them.

'I am travelling alone, and they allotted me a single cabin. A little past midnight, I heard someone snoring in the bunk above me,' one guest spoke in a hushed voice. 'I got up and found a sailor sleeping on the upper bunk. He was wearing a naval uniform. Just as I was about to seek help, the guy disappeared. I couldn't sleep the entire night.'

There was silence for a while as everyone grappled with the stories.

'The temperature in my cabin began dropping and soon, it was freezing. Suddenly, the heating came back. I don't know if it had anything to do with ghosts, but I have heard that the temperatures go down when there is paranormal activity in the area.'

'That must be it!' A man thumped his fist on the table, making everyone jump. He nodded at his wife and said, 'Our cabin was next to the sick bay, and we heard lots of eerie sounds through the night. When I got up to check, I saw an "orb" zipping past. It could probably be the spirits of the sailors who died of illness.'

'I don't believe in ghosts,' declared another guest. 'There's a perfectly good explanation for all the things that you have experienced. The authorities have converted this aircraft carrier into a tourist attraction. Tales of it being haunted have been spread, and they do their best to create a spooky atmosphere. Given the size and history of the craft, all it requires is a little imagination to make the guests believe ghosts were gallivanting around the ship.'

'It could probably be a few staff members, who carry on the charade by dressing up in uniforms and making eerie sounds,' Amar said, looking meaningfully at his wife. 'For instance, that guy Allen, whom you met, couldn't have been a ghost,' asserted Amar.

'Why not?' Roshni stuck out her chin. She liked the idea of having interacted with a ghost. She was keen on sharing the story with her friends in India.

'Ghosts don't talk like humans – I am sure of it.'

'That's what you think,' she snorted. 'It's easy to verify if Allen Smith is indeed a ghost. All we have to do is to check with the staff.'

'Let's do that.' Amar nodded. He was keen on dispelling his wife's belief.

Followed by a couple of curious guests, the two of them trooped up to the reception desk. 'Is there an employee named Allen Smith on board the ship?' Amar asked the lady behind the desk.

'One moment, please,' said the young woman. She tapped a few keys on the computer and nodded her head. 'Sorry, there is no such person.'

Amar turned to leave, but Roshni hesitated. She was excited at the way her story was shaping up. She had not written something this interesting for a long time, and this was sure to be commended by the editor. 'Is there an Allen Smith on the original crew list?'

'I will check,' the woman said, turning back to the computer and then replied, 'Yes, there was, but that was long ago.'

The couple looked at each other in surprise. 'How long ago did he work on the ship?' they asked almost simultaneously.

'Oh, it was a long time back, during the Second World War, if I remember correctly,' replied the lady. 'By the way, his daughter lives close by if you'd like to see her.'

'Could you give us her address?' Roshni asked on impulse. 'If it isn't a bother, of course!'

'It's no bother at all. She lives near 4th Street and Lincoln Avenue. It's not far, a fifteen-minute walk. Ask anyone there for the Smiths, and they will guide you to her house.'

'Don't tell me you intend to visit the Smiths!' Amar objected. 'Let's not waste any time. We have so much to see.'

'You don't understand, darling. This is an excellent story that can grab my editor's attention. I can't let this opportunity pass. It won't take much time. Please!'

It was late that morning when they checked out of the ship and knocked on the Smiths' door. An elderly lady of about eighty years of age opened the door and looked enquiringly at them. Before they could say anything, Roshni spotted a huge sepia photograph hanging on the living room wall. Clad in naval uniform, a cocky Allen Smith stared at her across the room. His handsome face wore an amused smile, eyes twinkled with mirth, as though he was enjoying the look of surprise on Roshni's face.

'It's him,' she whispered to Amar.

A few minutes later, seated in the living room, they listened to Patricia Smith's story. Her father, Allen, had been a pilot, flying one of the aircrafts on board the aircraft carrier. It was during the Second World War that the *USS Hornet*, after an exemplary performance and several successful strikes on the Japanese, ran into the eye of a storm somewhere off the coast of the Philippines and suffered severe damage. The storm damaged the flight decks and claimed over a hundred aircrafts that were on board the carrier. Most pilots went down with their airplanes. One of them was Allen Smith.

'5 June 1945 is an unforgettable day for the Smith family. My father died a brave man's death.' The old woman raised her head, and the couple saw a pair of tears rolling down her cheeks. 'He did us proud.'

'I met him last night,' Roshni said in a low voice. 'He was leading me to the washroom and vanished suddenly.'

'I have been told that he has been sighted walking around the ship. People say the carrier is haunted. I am not surprised. The *USS Hornet* was home to many sailors and staff, who died in action. What they don't understand is that the *Hornet* was my father's second home. He loved it and spent happy times on it with his colleagues. My father gave his life to save the *Hornet*. Isn't it natural for his spirit to roam the ship? None of the spirits onboard are evil,' Patricia said. 'They're all heroes.'

'I was lost and frightened,' confessed Roshni.

'Till date, no one has ever been hurt on the ship. In fact, there have been several cases when drunken people have been miraculously saved from falling overboard at night. My father was a kind man. He would hurt no one.'

'Thank you, Patricia, for sharing the story with us.' Amar got up and shook her hand. 'Your father must have been a great man.'

Roshni was excited about her story. 'I am a journalist and want to share your father's story with the readers back home in India. I hope you have no objection to my writing about Allen.'

At first, Patricia was hesitant, but Roshni was not one to give up. 'Think of it, Patricia. It will be a tribute to your father. I am sure he wouldn't have had any objections,' she said.

It took a little more pleading for the woman to agree.

'May I take a few pictures?' Roshni prodded. 'It will bring the story to life. I will send you a copy once it's printed.' The lady was gracious enough to agree to pose for a few pictures along with her father's photograph.

'I want to carry out an investigation,' declared Roshni as she stepped out of the Smith house. 'Paranormal incidents make wonderful stories. They excite the readers and the editors. My story is almost complete, but a couple of interviews would make it perfect.'

A bit of asking around led them to the offices of Alameda Paranormal Researchers. They delighted Roshni by sharing the details of the experiments they conducted onboard the *USS Hornet*. Using various meters, thermal imaging cameras, and maglite flashlights, the researchers discovered that the ship was haunted by the spirits of those who had died onboard during the Second World War. They shared a few stories about the ghostly happenings around the decks.

For Roshni, it turned out to be an unforgettable trip. Back home in Mumbai, she wrote a two-page story in the Sunday supplement of her newspaper, which garnered a lot of appreciation from readers. The editor was impressed, and Roshni found herself promoted.'

6

ONE NIGHT AT ABBOT MOUNT

Uday downed a glass of water and gnashed his teeth. These nonsensical stories were now exasperating him. For some strange reason, he felt chilled to the bone. Was it the effect of the spooky stories, he wondered?

'As you all know, I love hunting,' boomed a voice from across the table. 'And this story is better than all the hunting stories you have ever heard.'

Looking around, Uday noticed the muscular man with a Fedora sitting jauntily on his head. *Who wears such hats these days*? Uday smiled to himself as the man continued his story.

'Not far from Champawat, a small town in the foothills of the Himalayas in Uttarakhand, was a lovely place on top of a hill surrounded by thick forests. The tiny hamlet, in the thick forests of deodar and pine tree, lay at an altitude of 7000 feet. The most beautiful thing about the place was its magnificent view of the snow-capped peaks of the Himalayas. Exotic birds, butterflies, and wildlife completed the picture.

It wasn't surprising when the idyllic place became a place of choice for British officers during the Raj. Soon, the small hill town began flaunting luxurious bungalows and resembled an English village. An English businessman called John Harold Abbott had discovered the potential of this place.

An intrepid hiker, Abbott had been on one of his hiking trips when he had stumbled upon this little piece of heaven. Excited with his find, he had constructed a bungalow at the highest point of the hill. The year was 1914, and the idyllic bungalow was literally in the middle of nowhere. There were but a few scattered huts with local residents, who survived by cultivating the small patches of flat land and hunting in the surrounding forests. The place came to be known as Abbott Mount.

Word about the place soon spread. It was his love for hunting that drew George Smith to Abbott Mount. He was a daring hunter and a friend of Jim Corbett's. The abundance of wildlife was tempting enough for him to construct a bungalow at the sylvan location. It was an exciting life for the hunter who had accompanied Corbett on several hunting expeditions, during which the duo had had narrow escapes. Smith never ceased to boast about his escapades at the slightest opportunity. It made an excellent topic for conversation amongst hunting enthusiasts.

It was in 1917 that Smith finally retired and moved to his bungalow in Mount Abbott with his wife Elaine and two sons. By then, a few Englishmen who had heard about the place, bought land around Abbott's property and constructed a couple of bungalows. These remained unoccupied, with the owners planning to settle there in the future. The only time they occupied the bungalows was during the summers, when the heat and dust of the plains drove the British to the hills.

Winters in the Himalayan towns were harsh and living at Abbott Mount offered a challenge that few people were ready to accept. During the summer, big game was available in plenty for the handful of British residents who came to live in the area. The locals, who had lived in fear of the wild beasts, depended on the white men for their safety.

The villagers were quite used to smaller animals. It was the leopards and tigers, which killed their cattle, that worried them. Their anxiety mounted whenever a man-eater was spotted prowling around the place. The villagers avoided moving out of their houses during the evenings. Smith was good with his gun, and so the villagers sought his services whenever they spotted a leopard or a tiger.

The arrangement suited a man like Smith, who took pride in tracking down the beasts. The Smiths' bungalow with its sloping, tiled roof had four bedrooms with a spacious veranda running all around it. Well-manicured lawns, landscaped gardens, and arbours added to the surrounding natural beauty. The doors were double-layered and sturdy in order to provide protection from the wild animals that could be heard walking around the garden in the dead of night. The Smith boys, Timothy and Thomas, aged ten and twelve respectively, loved the hills, as did their parents. Save for the occasional danger of wild beasts, life was tranquil and satisfying.

In the summer of 1917, Captain Williams, who was recuperating after being wounded in the First World War, decided to spend some time with the Smiths. He was on sick leave and the doctors had advised him to spend a few weeks in the invigorating air of the hills. The two of them had attended the same school in England and were good friends. Their wives and children got along well with each other.

The Smiths were a hospitable family, and their bungalow had ample room to accommodate friends. They welcomed the opportunity to swap stories of war and the good times in England.

Timothy and Thomas were excited when they heard the Williams were coming to spend a few weeks at Abbott Mount. A couple of years ago, the two boys had spent a couple of days with Captain William's family and got along famously with their son, Frank, aged eleven. There was much excitement when the two families got together.

The boys were always outdoors during the day. They played cricket in the open grounds with the local boys, climbed trees and explored the area. The house was located at the edge of the jungle, and the boys were warned not to stray too far from the house, with the doors kept closed at all times.

Smith issued explicit instructions to everybody about the precautions to be taken. It was mandatory to remain indoors after sunset, and the two families spent the evening by playing cards, chess or listening to the stories narrated by the two men. Smith's hunting trips and William's war stories kept the boys engaged. Frank was fascinated by Smith's hunting exploits. He wanted to be a hunter like Jim Corbett and Smith, while Timothy wanted to go to war like Captain Williams.

The boys, like most boys their age, loved bragging. The Smith brothers boasted of having seen several snakes and wild animals. Carried away by their bravado, Frank declared he was not afraid of tigers, and he would kill man-eaters when he grew up.

'I don't believe you!' Timothy challenged Frank. 'Even brave men are afraid of man-eaters.'

'It's the truth. I am not afraid of tigers!' Frank said, refusing to back down. He wanted to impress the others with his boldness. 'I bet your father isn't afraid of man-eaters.'

'We'll know soon enough,' said Timothy. He was fed up with the chap's bragging.

The brothers decided to teach a lesson to Frank by playing a prank on him. It was a cold January night when the brothers decided to carry out their plan. Timothy and Frank were playing chess while, their parents were chatting and enjoying post dinner drinks in the drawing room.

Unseen by the others, Thomas crept out of the house with a box containing a tape recorder and amplifier. It was the tape recorder, on which Smith had recorded the sound of a tiger's roars. Although a beat of villagers was the preferred method to draw out a tiger or other wild animals, Smith often used the tape recorder for luring the wild beast out of its hideout successfully on several occasions.

Suddenly, there was a sound of shuffling in the shrubs outside. It was accompanied by the sound of a tiger's growling.

Realizing that Thomas had put their plan to action, Timothy suppressed a smile and watched Frank's reaction. The boy had paled on hearing the tiger's growls. He looked very frightened. Then, noticing that Timothy was watching his reaction, he forced a smile. After all his bragging, he couldn't afford to show he was scared.

But the boys were not the only ones who heard the tiger's growl. The adults had heard it too.

'Shhh! Quiet!' Smith whispered as he cocked his ears. There was pin-drop silence in the room. A couple of moments later, they heard it again. This time, it was clearer. Tension enveloped the room.

'What's it?' Elaine Smith stood up, spilling her coffee.

'Check the doors and windows, Elaine.' Smith got up and ran to fetch his gun. 'And fetch me a torch,' he instructed. 'I think the man-eater is on the prowl.'

'Is it in the garden?' asked Williams.

'It sounded close by. Don't worry, I'll get it tonight.'

By then, Frank was shivering with fright. Timothy smiled. The loudmouth would never dare to brag again.

'You can't go alone. I'll come with you,' offered Captain Williams as Smith emerged from the bedroom with his gun.

'No! I don't want you to limp around, offering yourself as a meal to the bloodthirsty beast,' Smith said and took the torch from Elaine. 'Just stay here and remain quiet,' he said in a low voice. 'I'll be back in a jiffy.'

There was a tangible feeling of terror in the room. Captain Williams stood rooted to the spot, wringing his hands helplessly. He had faced guns and enemies in war, but man-eating tigers were an entirely different matter. He had no expertise in hunting wild beasts.

Violet Williams held tight to her husband's hand, preventing him from going out with Smith. She began praying softly. Timothy watched in satisfaction as Frank curled up on the sofa, his hands clutching at the cushions for support. The prank was working wonderfully.

Timothy was in two minds as he watched his father walking towards the door with the gun in his hand. He was enjoying Frank's distress and did not want the trick to end so soon. But he had to stop his father from stepping out of the house. His father would shoot and Thomas, who was outside, could be shot dead.

'Don't go out, Dad. Th ... there is n ... no man-eater. It's a ... a joke. It could be Thomas playing the tape recorder,' he stammered. He was afraid of his father's vile temper, but he was more afraid of the danger his brother faced.

'What? Bloody hell! What are you saying?' An enraged Smith began to shake his younger son. 'That's not the tape recorder – that's a real tiger. Where is Thomas?' he shouted.

'He ... he is out there p ... p ... playing the tape.'

'Get the hell out of my way!' Smith pushed Timothy out of the way and rushed out. He was just in time to see the tiger leaping into of the bushes and disappearing. He fired two quick shots. The sound echoed in the surrounding hills, and then there was silence.

The dying echo of the gunshots roused the villagers. With lit mashaals, they emerged cautiously from their huts and gathered at the Smith bungalow. Amazed, they watched Smith hunting for his son in a crazed manner. The tape recorder and amplifier lay under a tree, but Thomas was nowhere to be found.

There was chaos inside the bungalow. Violet Williams was trying to console Elaine Smith, who was crying uncontrollably. Frank was curled up on the sofa, mumbling incoherently, and Timothy stood dumbfounded in one corner of the veranda. Captain Williams shouted for help. He instructed the villagers to go in search of Thomas.

The villagers, their path lit up by burning mashaals, looked around for Thomas all around the forest that night. They shouted his name until their voices turned hoarse, but they did not find the boy. Dawn was breaking as they returned home, dejected by their failure. The man-eater had claimed several lives, and they lived in perpetual fear of losing more. The only thing they knew was that the beast had to be eliminated at the earliest. They would have to wait for Smith sahib to get over his grief before proposing that he kill the tiger.

Gloom descended on the Smith household. Not a drop of water passed into Elaine's mouth, and Smith was inconsolable. Timothy was in a state of shock. Never had he imagined that a harmless prank would turn into a fatal accident, claiming his brother's life.

Captain William and his wife took charge of the bungalow and its residents, coaxing the Smiths to eat. Thomas's body had not been found, and Elaine Smith refused to accept that her son was dead.

'Tom is alive,' she insisted. 'He's hiding in the forest – I want you to look for him.'

Nothing Smith said could convince her that the tiger had killed Thomas. Finally, it was for her satisfaction that Smith set out into the forest. This time, he took expert trackers from the village, and they ventured deeper into the jungle. The sun rode overhead as they searched each patch of the dense forest, looking for clues and remains. They found the remains of the earlier victims who had fallen prey to the man-eater.

The man-eater, who the villagers had named Shamshera, had taken several lives before disappearing for a long time. They assumed it had died, but it returned just as they had heaved a sigh of relief. Its last victim had been a teenaged girl called Chandra. She had gone to the forest to gather firewood and had never returned. Under a large banyan tree, the villagers found the black shawl she had been wearing, stained with her blood. They also found her anklet near the tree, which seemed to be Shamshera's favourite haunt.

Chandra had been killed a few months ago, and then the man-eater disappeared. It was rumoured that her spirit had chased away Shamshera and was protecting the villagers. But now, the tiger had returned, and Thomas was its first prey that year. The incident put fear back in the hearts of the locals.

An exhausted Smith sat despondently under the massive banyan tree. It was past noon, and they had been searching for over six hours. The villagers stood respectfully at a distance, talking in low voices. Just then, they heard a whimper. Their ears cocked, the men looked around fearfully. Smith picked up his gun, which had been resting against the tree trunk. His senses heightened; the hunter prepared to shoot. And then he heard a feeble cry. Looking up into the tree, he spotted Thomas, half hidden in the foliage. The frightened boy was sitting on a sturdy branch.

'Tom!' Smith could barely control his tears as he quickly climbed the tree. 'Don't worry! Dad is here,' he shouted.

A couple of minutes later, assisted by the villagers, Smith brought down his son. Thomas was shivering, and his body was burning with fever.

There was jubilation when the hunter returned home. Elaine could not hold back her tears as she rocked her son and thanked God for keeping him safe. Smith rewarded the villagers and sent them away. Timothy, who had not spoken a word or eaten since the disappearance of his brother, smiled with relief. He tousled Tom's hair and hugged him, whispering, 'No more pranks, Tom. You had us worried.'

Three days passed before the shocked boy recovered. The fever receded, but fear had stilled his tongue. Smith questioned him again and again, but there was no explanation for what had happened. How had he reached the banyan tree that night? What happened to the tiger? There were a dozen questions that troubled his mind. But Thomas refused to speak. Fear gripped him each time his father mentioned the man-eater.

In the meantime, the villagers discussed the boy's miraculous escape. There was something unreal about the whole affair. But the man-eater had still not been killed. It was sure to return and claim some more lives, and the villagers remained on tenterhooks.

A week passed and then two. Then one night, the villagers heard the unmistakable roar of the man-eater. It was the roar of a wounded beast intent on revenge. Terrified, they rushed to Smith's bungalow. The man-eater had returned. The villagers wanted Smith to kill the man-eater so they could live in peace. The hunter, enraged at the tiger's attack on his family, was equally determined to shoot the animal.

It was late afternoon when Smith set out with a group of beaters. The entire village rallied around him. They carried spears, daggers, swords, and iron rods. So enraged were they that they entered the forest from many directions to direct the animals toward Smith, who was lying in wait.

Deer cowered, monkeys chattered and birds started flying fearfully around the forest as the villagers converged with their mashaals, making a din. Many animals emerged from the forest, but the man-eating tiger refused to be cornered. It was around 4 p.m. when they heard the roar of the enraged beast. But it was nowhere to be seen. The trees were large, the foliage thick and the undergrowth copious. Visibility was poor in the area from where the beast had been heard. No one dared to go close, for it could prove fatal. The tiger could spring out and pounce, killing anyone who ventured close.

The waiting game continued. Smith was about fifty meters away from the banyan tree, but the tiger could still not be seen. He realized that any further delays would be useless because soon it would get dark and they would have to return without killing the man-eater.

With the rifle held steady in his hands, he advanced slowly in the direction of the growling. Step by step, he progressed, his eyes unblinking and focused. In the forest, it is believed that a hunter may not see the animal, but the animal always sees you.

Tension grew as the villagers watched, ready to spring to Smith's defence. Smith was now about twenty meters away from the massive banyan tree. There was silence as he continued to advance, slowly and stealthily.

All of a sudden, there was a deep snarl. Its jaw wide open and fangs bared, the tiger leapt out of the bushes and at the hunter. But Smith was prepared. He fired, and the tiger dropped dead at his feet. The bullet went through its open mouth, and out of its head from the rear, shattering its brain. No one had ever seen such a shot or heard of one. Jubilant, the villagers carried Smith on their shoulders, dancing all the way back to Mount Abbott. They strung the man-eater on bamboo poles and carried it to the bungalow. Its skin would adorn the floor of the Smiths' drawing room.

Later, the villagers would boast about Smith's hunting skills. It became an account that was repeated in hunting circles with awe. Smith had shot right into the tiger's mouth as it came charging at him. It was a rare feat, achieved by very few hunters in the world. That incident established Smith's credentials as one of the best hunters in that region of India.

As for Thomas, the boy finally broke his silence at the sight of the dead tiger. The Smith family, along with Captain William and the children, were celebrating when Tom said, 'I am happy Shamshera is dead. It would have killed me if Chandra had not saved me that night.'

Aghast, they listened to Thomas's story. 'I had just switched on the tape recorder when the tiger arrived. It leapt at me, and I swooned in fear. I don't know what happened after that. All I know is that I felt myself being pulled by someone, and we were racing through the jungle pursued by the man-eater. My feet barely touched the ground. I floated. We finally reached the banyan tree, and I found myself on a sturdy branch while the tiger lay in a stunned state underneath.'

Elaine patted his hands as the boy trembled at the memory. 'I was shaking all over and crying. Then the girl—she said her name was Chandra—stroked my hair and held me till I felt better. She told me that the tiger would go away, and I should remain where I was. "Nothing will happen to you," she said. "Don't worry, your father will be here tomorrow."'

It was an incredible story. Smith, who did not believe in ghosts, found it hard to give credence to his son's account. But how had Tom reached the banyan tree, which was miles away from the bungalow, he wondered? There was no doubt that Thomas had had a miraculous escape, and some supernatural power had been at work. Elaine had no doubt, nor had Timothy. They were sure it was Chandra's spirit that saved Tom from the jaws of death.

On Elaine's insistence, they constructed a shrine under the banyan tree on which they found Thomas. It was her homage to Chandra's ghost. There has not been a single death because of any man-eater at Mount Abbott since that day. Every year on the date of Chandra's death, villagers congregate to pray at the temple, which is now called the Bagh Devi Temple.'

'Does the temple still exist?' asked Keshavmama. 'Mount Abbot must be a beautiful place. I would love to visit the place! Uday, would you like to accompany me to Mount Abbot, or are you in a hurry to get back to your job?'

'Some other time maybe,' Uday responded. He was half asleep in his chair and wished the round of stories would end. But that was not to be as the next person had begun speaking.

7

THE SPOOKY GALLOWS

'My story is about a friendly ghost,' announced a voice from the other end of the table.

'There is nothing like a friendly ghost!' Uday snapped. 'All ghost stories are about scary ghosts.'

The grating voice of the man was getting on his already frazzled nerves.

'You don't believe there are amicable ghosts? challenged a man wearing a suit. 'I assure you, not all ghosts are vindictive or violent.'

'Let me decide after you narrate your story.' Uday wished the fellow would proceed with the story instead of wasting time.

'Yes, let's hear the story,' clamoured a few voices.

'It was an election year, and as with every election, this one also saw feverish activity and many violent incidents. Violent incidents were on the rise as were criminal activities. The prisons were getting crowded as the police went into overdrive. In the capital, an important person was murdered, and three suspects were put behind bars in Tihar Jail. They had been caught at the railway station. Among them was a man named Pawan, who was returning to Delhi after attending his grandfather's funeral in his village. Unwilling to miss the late night train, he boarded it without buying a ticket.

Fate caught up with Pawan when he alighted at the New Delhi Railway Station. To his misfortune, someone in the crowd had planted a gun in his backpack, the very weapon that had been used for the murder. He had no idea how it came into his possession, but the police refused to believe him. Pawan was stunned. He had assumed that he was being arrested for ticketless travel but found himself charged with the murder of a politician.

The poor chap had no money, and his phone had been stolen during the journey, so he could not inform his parents or seek anyone's help. After a flurry of court procedures, the magistrate remanded him in custody along with the two other men, accused of the same murder.

Pawan found himself in Tihar Jail No. 4, along with other undertrials. As against the sanctioned capacity of 6,250 prisoners, the Tihar Jail housed over 10,000 inmates. So, some of the hardened criminals were housed with the under-trials and this resulted in several unpleasant incidents.

Jail No. 4 of the Tihar Jail, where Pawan was crammed in with several criminals, was a miserable place with a nauseating smell of sweat and stale food. Helpless and dejected, Pawan began weeping till he was exhausted. It was midnight by the time he fell asleep. Suddenly, he was awakened by a stinging slap. Everyone seemed to be asleep. Who had slapped him, he wondered, looking around the cell. Then he saw a man standing near the bars. Dressed in white, the fellow wagged a finger warningly, as though scolding him for some wrong deed. Suddenly, the man vanished as suddenly as he had appeared.

Pawan had dozed off when he heard another slap ringing in the dark. The slap was followed by loud cursing. The sounds were coming from the adjoining cell. He wondered what was happening. Was this a nightly ritual or a practical joke being played by another prisoner?

The next morning, Pawan lined up with the other prisoners for breakfast. Most of them had spent quite some time in jail and knew their way around. One of them, Kishanlal, who seemed to be the gang leader, snatched away his food, and everyone laughed. He cringed with fear as Kishanlal threatened him with dire consequences if he complained to the guards.

'Why are you bullying the poor fellow? Find someone your own size,' said a strapping man, rebuking the bully. Taking pity on the puny Pawan, he pulled the hapless guy to the side and shared his meal.

'You will have to deal with bullies like Kishanlal,' said the man, whose name was Lakhan Singh. 'You can't let them take away your food. After a while, they won't stop at food. They will subject you to all kinds of demeaning tasks.'

'I am frightened,' admitted Pawan, tears flowing down his face. 'I have never been to a prison.'

Lakhan Singh patted his arm consolingly. He pitied the anxious man, who didn't look like a criminal. 'You will soon learn, and I will help you.' They ate in silence for a couple of minutes. 'Why were you brought here? What did you do?'

There was sympathy in the man's voice, and Pawan broke down. Haltingly, he narrated his tragic story. 'I would have missed the night train if I had queued up to buy a ticket. I work as a daily wager in a factory. I will go hungry if I lose a single day's wages. Ironically, I was arrested at the railway station with a gun, of which I had no knowledge. I am not in jail for ticketless travelling but for a crime I didn't commit.'

Lakhan Singh, who had spent many months in the prison, had been caught for dacoity. In those months, he had seen several young men being imprisoned, but most claimed to be innocent. This one actually looked too meek to murder anyone. He couldn't even protect his food from a bully like Kishanlal.

'Have faith! If you are innocent, the judge will set you free. All you need is a good lawyer.'

'But I don't have any money – no one will fight my case.'

The burly man had no words to console the distraught fellow. He was aware of several poor men who languished in jail forever because they could not afford a good lawyer. 'Well, miracles do happen!' Lakhan mumbled.

Pawan wondered if he should tell Lakhan about the slapping incident. He spoke after a brief hesitation. 'A weird incident took place last night. Someone slapped me while I was sleeping. I looked around, but everyone was sleeping. A little later, there was the sound of slapping followed by loud curses. It was quite frightening. I was too scared to sleep after that,' he confided as they walked along with the others towards the jail factory.

'That's strange! It may have been a nightmare. Such things happen when one is upset, you know.'

Lakhan's explanation failed to convince Pawan. He could still feel the sting of the slap on his right cheek, and he'd understood the curses he'd heard. He couldn't have imagined it all. The strapping criminal tried to brush them off, but Pawan was insistent. The sounds had been quite distinct. He sensed that the other man was being evasive.

Just then, Lakhan was informed that he had visitors. 'It must be my wife. She brings me food sometimes,' he grinned. 'I don't want to miss home food. Go ahead with Patil. He doesn't speak much, but he's a dependable man,' said Lakhan, pointing at a man walking ahead.

'Okay, I need friends in my corner,' Pawan smiled and began walking towards Patil. He turned back as an idea hit him. He borrowed a pen from a nearby guard, and wrote his father's mobile number on Lakhan's palm. 'I am sure your wife will have a piece of paper or something on which she can copy the phone number.' He stole a look around and continued, 'Please tell your wife to call this number and inform my father about what has happened. I am sorry for the bother, but my parents must be worried as they haven't heard from me.'

'It's not a problem,' said the burly man, and patted Pawan's shoulder reassuringly. 'She'll find a way to make the call. Don't worry.'

Eager to make a new friend, Pawan quickened his pace and joined Patil. His warm smile vanished as Patil greeted him with a sullen look.

'Have you been here for long?' Pawan asked, trying to break the ice.

'Two years.'

Pawan tried again. 'You must be familiar with everything.' The statement brought forth a grunt from Patil. Unfazed, Pawan continued, 'Lakhan Singh is the only person who has spoken to me.'

'No one is here to socialize,' said Patil, curling his lips menacingly.

That put an end to the conversation for a while as they walked in silence for a distance. But Pawan was unwilling to give up. He was an inquisitive man, so he continued questioning Patil about the buildings, areas, and complexes they passed on the way.

'Can't a man walk in peace?' Patil snarled and stopped in his tracks.

'Sorry! I didn't want to annoy you, but ...'

'But what?'

'One last question. What is that building?' Pawan pointed at a building on their left.

Patil ignored the question and quickened his pace. Not just that, he refused to look at the building Pawan was pointing to. He tried his best to shake off the pestering fellow.

Pawan, however, kept asking questions. He continued to follow the man doggedly.

'That is Jail No. 3,' Patil said, at last, refusing to look at the building. He had realized it was impossible to avoid Pawan's questions. 'Keep away from it,' he added warningly.

Perplexed, Pawan walked in silence till they reached the jail factory area. He couldn't help asking why as they walked to their assigned area of work.

'That's the Phansi Kothi – the place you'll go to be hanged,' Patil snapped. 'Now stop bothering me and get to work.'

Although the words sent a chill down his spine, Pawan was curious to know about the place. Did they still hang murderers? When was the last hanging? There were a dozen questions in his mind. Patil was not forthcoming, so he decided to ask Lakhan during lunch.

'Brother, you better forget about that complex. It brings nothing but bad luck, especially while eating. Why don't we speak of pleasant things?' said Lakhan, trying to divert Pawan's attention.

The word Phansi Kothi reminded Lakhan of the hanging of a militant a week after he had been imprisoned. There had been a lot of commotion before and after the hanging, and many prisoners had reported seeing the militant's ghost loitering around Jail Nos. 3 and 4. 'My wife has promised to call your parents today.'

'Thank you, Lakhan.'

'Don't thank me, brother. Come and give me a box of sweets after you are released.'

'Do you think I will be released?' Pawan's eyes were shining with excitement at the prospect of going home.

'I am confident you will be set free. You are a nice young man, and the judge would have to be blind not to see that.'

Pawan was presented at the court the next morning. The magistrate, a bored-looking man, snapped at the lawyer for not putting up a proper case. He postponed the hearing for another day and sent the prisoners back to the jail. It was a disappointment for Pawan, and he discussed the matter with his fellow prisoners, who told him it was quite rare to be set free so soon. He would have to go to the court till the magistrate was convinced of his innocence.

'Why don't you forget about the court and the case?' chuckled Satnam, a fellow convicted for theft. A habitual offender, he seemed to enjoy his stay in the prison. 'Don't worry too much. Just enjoy the free food and the prison's hospitality while you are here.'

Despite the advice, Pawan was uncomfortable with his sentence. 'I did no wrong,' he continued to insist.

'You wouldn't be here if you did no wrong,' Satnam smirked. 'Don't keep snivelling around me. I hate a crybaby!' he said, landing a kick on Pawan's backside. 'Get me some water.'

A couple of days passed, but Pawan continued to be haunted by a morbid curiosity about the Phansi Kothi. He stared at the place each time they passed and would not be satisfied till he had received answers to his questions.

'What do you want to know about the cursed place?' Lakhan asked irritably when he raked up the topic one evening.

'I want to know all about it.'

'There have been several hangings in the gallows in that place. I haven't seen it, nor do I wish to ever see it. What I know has come from the other prisoners. The path from Jail No. 3

leads directly to the gallows where terrorists, murderers and rapists have been hanged. The cells inside Jail No. 3, are where the high-risk convicts are locked up. I have heard that the terrorist Afzal Guru, convicted for the attack on parliament, was held there, and some prisoners have reported being visited by the ghosts of Ranga and Billa. There are dozens of stories and many rumours, and no one knows the truth. Does this information satisfy you or are you going to go around hunting for more?'

'I am sorry to have upset you, Lakhan,' Pawan apologized. He noticed that the brawny man was visibly distressed. 'I ...'

'Please!' Lakhan held up a hand. 'No more questions about that place. It's a bad omen to talk about the gallows, and there's enough stress without it. Patil is expecting a death sentence, and so are some other prisoners. All this talk will only upset them, and you may be beaten up if you continue.' There was silence for a while and then he asked, 'Do you believe in ghosts?'

'I haven't seen one. But everyone in my village talks about ghosts. There are supposed to be a few living in the banyan tree near the pond,' Pawan said.

'Before you ask, let me tell you that the slapping incident you experienced is nothing but the ghosts revisiting their cell.'

'I wondered ...'

'There's nothing to wonder. The criminals who were hanged often visit the cell where they spent their last days.'

Fear kept Pawan from sleeping that night. He tossed on his thin mat, uncomfortable after the discussion about ghosts. What if the ghost slapped or strangled him as he slept? And Lakhan's warning about upsetting the prisoners still stayed with him. It was true that he had been asking too many questions about the Phansi Kothi. What if Patil or the others decided to beat him up?

By then, he had learned enough about the violence that took place in the cells. He had seen too many broken bones and bruises, some of which had landed some prisoners in the hospital. The prisoners were a violent lot. Any minor matter could become a trigger for a severe beating. All he wanted was to go home.

Curling himself into a ball, he lay in the dark, worrying about ghosts and his fellow prisoners. The cell was filled with the sound of loud snores and farts. At last, he fell into a restless slumber.

Pawan woke up with a start. Someone had tapped him on the shoulder. He sprang to his feet and looked at the skeletal man standing before him. Covered in a white sheet, he seemed seven feet tall. A skull with a pair of empty sockets stared back at him. Pawan didn't have to be told it was a ghost. Was this the ghost that had slapped him? Expecting a slap, his hands flew to his cheeks.

'Don't worry, nothing will happen to you,' said a hollow and chilling voice that seemed to come from a distance. 'The magistrate will issue orders to free you after your court appearance tomorrow.' Saying this, the ghostly figure turned to go.

Pawan felt faint. His legs were trembling, but he willed himself to keep standing. There were so many questions in his mind. He wanted to ask why he had been slapped the other day, but his tongue remained frozen. Helplessly, he watched the ghost melt through the iron bars and disappear.

It was only after the ghost had gone that Pawan could move. He rushed towards the iron bars on the door of the cell and in the bargain, he banged his head against the bars and collapsed.

The prisoners noticed the bump on his forehead the next morning. They assumed he had been roughed up by one of his cellmates. Lakhan was furious.

'Just tell me the name of the person who has done this to you, and I will do the rest,' he said.

'I fell against the iron bars and hit my head.'

'Don't try to fool me,' shouted Lakhan. 'No one falls against the iron bars at night. Why are you trying to protect the bully? Do you think he'll stop thrashing you because you're being protective?'

'I am telling the truth, Lakhan. No one thrashed me. I fell down. You may find it hard to believe, but a very strange thing happened last night,' said Pawan, lowering his voice. 'I had just fallen asleep when someone tapped me on the shoulder.'

'Now, you are going to insist that it was a ghost who hit you on the head,' Lakhan sneered. Amused at the story, he began guffawing. 'I am not a child, Pawan.'

'I am telling you what happened. You can choose not to believe it, of course.'

'All right, please continue your fairy tale.'

'The ghost told me that the magistrate will issue an order to set me free today. If you recall, I am to be presented at the court this morning. Let's see if the ghost is right.'

'So, what did the ghost look like? Did you see him?'

'Of course! I saw him clearly.'

'What did he look like?'

'He was covered in white, and he had empty sockets where his eyes should have been. I was terrified.' Pawan shuddered as he recalled the ghost.

'Rubbish! You will be back in this cell by afternoon.'

Pawan believed the ghost's prediction and remained optimistic about his release. It took just a few minutes for the magistrate to give his decision. He was set free after a stern warning against travelling without a ticket. He would have to pay a penalty, he was told.

'He was right – I am to be released!' Pawan announced to Lakhan after returning to the cell. He hugged his protector and danced around. 'You didn't believe me when I told you the truth. What do you have to say now?'

'I don't know!' Lakhan shook his head. 'It's so uncanny.'

After his release from the Tihar Jail, Pawan went back to his village. He narrated the story, but very few people believed him. A ghost predicting good things? they mocked. He didn't care.

Years passed. Pawan is now an old man, but the memory of the ghost remains fresh in his mind. He continues to narrate the story to his grandchildren, who are the only ones that believe him.

'You have told us that the ghost was friendly. But Dadaji, my friends say ghosts are evil,' said the seven-year-old.

'No, my child, not all of them are evil. Just like humans, there are good as well as evil ghosts. Like you, I also believed that they were evil, but the friendly ghost proved me wrong. Everything is not black or white. There are grey shades in between.' Pawan laughed. Unlike most humans, Pawan doesn't fear ghosts.'

The storyteller looked around for appreciation.

'That's exactly my point,' Keshavmama raised his voice to drown the babble of comments. 'Not all ghosts are evil.'

'That was a wonderful story,' bellowed a pompous voice. 'But I think I have a better one.'

'Why not allow us to be a judge of that?' chuckled Keshavmama.

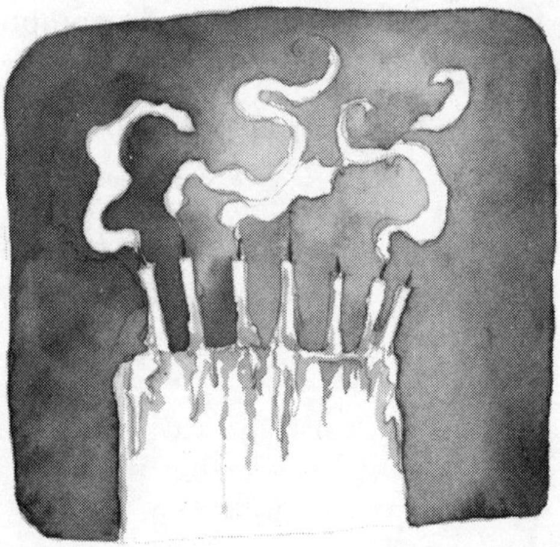

8

THE BIRTHDAY GIRL

'Having served in the army, I have travelled across the length and breadth of the country. Let me tell you, I know dozens of ghost stories,' said the stout man seated next to Uday. His military moustache bristled with excitement at the prospect of narrating his story. 'The one I am about to narrate took place right in the heart of the capital.'

Clearing his throat importantly, the fellow began his story.

'It had been only a week since Captain Sameer Kulkarni had been posted to a unit in Delhi. It seemed godsent after the two harrowing years he had spent in a terrorist-infested outpost in Kashmir. He had yet to get over the excitement of staying in a city with dazzling malls and restaurants that offered all kinds of cuisine. Each evening was an opportunity to catch up with the pleasures he had missed for two full years. Escaping the freezing temperatures of the Kashmir Valley was also a reason to rejoice. Fond of driving, the officer had missed the opportunity to do so during his last tenure because security reasons prohibited army personnel from going out on their own. He now rejoiced in zooming around on his Royal Enfield motorcycle.

Not just Sameer, his parents, who had been engaged in finding a suitable daughter-in-law, were happy that their son could finally find the time to get married. His mother was sure that her tall, brawny handsome son deserved the best possible wife, and the hunt had been going on for a long while. Sameer was amused by her persistence.

One Saturday evening, he had decided to finish a couple of chores after a game of tennis. One of his colleagues was throwing a party to celebrate his wedding anniversary the next evening, and he had yet to buy a gift. Buying gifts was an unpleasant task for the young officer as he could never decide on an appropriate item to suit the occasion. Determined to finish the task at hand, he stopped to withdraw some cash from an ATM.

'Might as well get it done,' he mumbled as he mounted his motorcycle and headed towards a gift shop in Gopinath Bazar. After much dilly-dallying, he put off the purchase till the next evening. *I will buy a bottle of expensive wine*, he decided. All he bought then were a few chocolates for the colleague's two-year-old daughter.

It was getting dark as he drove towards his room in the Officers' Mess. Sameer was passing a dimly lit patch on a lonely road when he saw a woman standing on the kerb. Balancing a package in her left hand, she gestured with the thumb of her right hand, requesting a lift. He slowed down and hesitated. Having heard stories about the nefarious activities that sometimes took place in that area, he was reluctant to stop.

As he neared the woman, he realized she was young and attractive. Her sari hugged a shapely figure, and she exuded sensuality. Should he drive away, he wondered. Refusing to help a woman in trouble was against his nature, and the chivalrous officer decided to ask a few questions before he gave her a ride.

'How can I help you, ma'am?' he asked.

'I have been waiting here for the past twenty minutes, but not a single autorickshaw has passed this way. Could you please drop me at Mehar Marg, please? I am in a hurry, and this place is too deserted for me to feel safe.'

For a split second, he wondered what she was doing there. Was it a trap? It would be safer to ignore her and keep driving. But … would it be right to forsake a woman in distress? What if she really needed his help?

Sameer looked around, unable to reach a decision, but then gallantry reared its head.

Realising his hesitation, she said, 'My name is Arati Khanna, and I'm the daughter of Air Commodore Naveen Khanna.

I hope that information will help you decide if you want to help me.'

Embarrassed by her jibe, he replied, 'I'm sorry that I appeared reluctant. I will drop you home. Let me hold your package while you get on the bike.'

'Be careful, it is my birthday, and this is the cake,' she said, handing over the box to Sameer.

'Happy birthday!' he smiled at his pillion rider as he handed the box back. She was beautiful, he realized as he gazed at her closely. 'Do I get a piece of cake?'

'It depends on how well you behave,' she said, putting a hand on his shoulder. Suddenly, he felt cold and shivered.

It was a short drive to her house. Five minutes later, regretting that the drive had ended so soon, he held the package as she clambered down. Arati smiled and vanished down the short pathway that led to her house, leaving him still holding the package. He waved his right hand in a dazed manner as she disappeared inside the house. *What a charming girl. I should have asked for her phone number*, he mused.

A minute later, realizing that she had forgotten the cake, he hastened across the lawn and rang the doorbell of Air Commodore Naveen Khanna's house. He was stumped by the sudden happenings of the evening. Would the Khannas invite him to the party, he wondered as he stood on the doorstep.

But something seemed a little weird. The house seemed too quiet to be having a party, and there were no vehicles parked around the house. Just then, a woman opened the door and stared questioningly at him. Her eyes were red and puffy, he noticed.

A little flustered, Sameer held out the package saying, 'Good evening, ma'am. I am sorry to disturb you, but Arati forgot her birthday cake.'

'Birthday cake?' she said, seeming shocked. She shrank back from the cake, as though terrified.

'Who is it, Nilima?' A man appeared behind her.

'I ... I ... don't know.' She broke into loud sobs and rushed inside the house.

Flabbergasted at the strange behaviour of the Khanna family, Sameer wondered if he should leave the cake at the doorstep and drive away.

'Who are you, young man?' asked Commodore Khanna.

'My name is Captain Sameer Kulkarni. Your daughter, Arati, requested me to drop her home and told me it was her birthday. Unfortunately, she forgot to take the cake,' said Sameer, holding out the package.

'You better come in,' said the Commodore curtly.

There was no trace of any party or guests, and nor was Arati around. Sameer ran his eyes over the tastefully decorated living room. *It's so weird*, thought the young officer. There was no sign of celebration. Instead, the house seemed in mourning. Perhaps there had been a sad incident in the family.

'Will you have tea?' asked the Commodore after Sameer took his seat.

'No, thank you, sir. I have to get back to the Officers' Mess.' But he was curious to know the reason for Mrs Khanna's odd behaviour.

'Tell me, where did you meet Arati and what did she tell you?' said the Commodore, his eyes boring into Sameer. 'Narrate everything, without skipping any details.'

Doesn't he believe me? Suddenly, Sameer wanted to walk away and have nothing to do with the family, but his curiosity got the better of him. There was something afoot, and he wanted to know what it was. Besides, he hoped to meet Arati again. He decided to humour the father.

'Well, I was driving back to the Officers' Mess when I passed a deserted road where I found Arati waiting for transportation. She told me she had been waiting for a while and requested me to give her a lift. It was her birthday, she said. I was hesitant, but the place was quite deserted and dimly lit. It didn't seem safe to leave her stranded, so I gave her a ride. I dropped her at your gate and was turning to go when I realized she had forgotten her birthday cake.'

'Are you sure it was Arati?'

'Sir, I have never met the lady so I can't say with any conviction,' Sameer said testily. Normally a patient man, he was beginning to get annoyed. 'I am going by what she said. She guided me to this house and told me she was the daughter of Air Commodore Khanna. I have no way of verifying the statement. You can't hold me responsible if she was lying.'

'Was this the girl who asked you for a ride?' the Commodore asked, showing him a picture of a girl.

'That's the one.'

'I mean no offense, young man, and I am sorry to grill you in this manner, but I have a sound reason for doing it.' The Commodore spread his hands helplessly. His shoulders drooping, the senior officer looked weary. For a few minutes, an uncomfortable silence hung between the two men as the Commodore grappled with his emotions. 'You will understand my reasons once I narrate my part of the story,' he finally said.

Watching the flitting emotions on the Commodore's face, Sameer felt his resentment draining. He was about to ask a few questions when they were joined by the Commodore's wife, who brought tea.

'Can you tell me where exactly you met Arati?' asked Mrs Khanna, her eyes misting with unshed tears. 'What was the time and what was she wearing?'

Sameer answered her queries patiently, wondering why she wanted to know those details. She listened to his response and started crying again.

'May I leave, sir?' Unable to bear the heavy gloom that hung like a thick dark curtain, the young officer got up to go.

'Wait! Don't you want to know everything?' the Commodore began. 'Arati died in a road accident a month ago. It was a hit-and-run case – she was only twenty-four.'

Sameer was shocked. '*What*? Was the driver arrested?' he asked.

'The accident took place on the same deserted road you describe. Unfortunately, there were no witnesses, and the police never found the driver. The case has not been closed, but we have little hope of the culprit being nabbed,' Arati's father said, staring at his feet dejectedly.

Mrs Khanna sat sobbing softly by her husband's side. 'My daughter died so young. She was so beautiful and talented,' she said, looking at Sameer for understanding. 'Arati was studying to be a surgeon. We had so many plans for her – we'd hoped to get her married this year.' She blew her nose gently.

Shaken, Sameer stared at the photograph of the girl. If Arati was dead, who was the woman he had dropped at the Khannas' residence, he wondered. *Did I give a ghost a ride*? The thought made him shudder. He didn't believe in ghosts, but this was something that had actually happened to him. He couldn't deny the incident.

Sameer had heard many ghost stories during his childhood. He had been told that people who died abnormal deaths sometimes became ghosts because their spirit remained discontented. Those murdered turned into ghosts to take revenge. But Arati had not harmed him – she only wanted a ride. In fact, by leading him to her house, she had given him a chance to console her parents.

'I am sorry for your loss,' he said, getting to his feet. 'I will leave my phone number with you. Please let me know if there is anything I can do.' This time, they didn't stop him.

Sameer had reached near the door when Mrs Khanna said, 'Can you do me a favour?'

'Sure, ma'am,' he said, pausing at the door as he turned to look at her.

'Please take me to the place where she asked you for a ride.' She looked at him pleadingly.

'Give me a moment, and I will come with you,' said the Commodore.

Minutes later, the three of them set out for the spot where he had seen Arati. The Khannas followed Sameer in their car. It took them a few minutes to reach the spot, and Sameer stopped his bike and pointed to where he'd seen their daughter. It turned out to be the exact spot where she had been mowed down by a car.

It was an emotional moment for the Khannas, and Mrs Khanna was inconsolable. 'I want the culprit punished,' she cried. 'My daughter's soul will not be at peace till he his.'

Her husband remained rooted to the spot for a couple of moments. It was embarrassing for Sameer to watch them struggling with their emotions. 'May I leave?' he asked Commodore Khanna.

'Thank you, young man. I will take my wife home.'

Relieved, Sameer rode away on his motorcycle. That night, as he went over the events of the evening, sleep remained elusive. Although disturbed by the happenings, his mind refused to accept he had met Arati's ghost. How was that possible? He didn't believe in ghosts and all that paranormal stuff. But the officer decided that the matter needed investigation.

Would Arati revisit the spot? He wanted to see if she would ask him for a ride once again.

With that in mind, Sameer traversed the same route at the same time the next Saturday. The deserted road lay in darkness; the streetlight was flickering moodily, and the moon had not risen. He drove slowly, looking all around, hoping to see Arati. And sure enough, he spotted her approaching from the opposite direction. It was the very spot where he had met her before. Coming closer, she waved at him. He stopped near her but kept the engine running. 'Arati Khanna. Right?' he asked. 'You want me to drop you home?'

'No, I am going to Gopinath Bazar.'

'Your parents are very distressed – why don't you speak to your mother?'

'I don't want her to be upset, but there's nothing I can do.'

'Your mother wants the culprit to be arrested and punished. She may find peace if he is put behind bars.'

'That's up to the police,' she replied, turning to leave.

'Wait!' Sameer shouted. 'Don't go! There's a lot you can do. You can lead me to the criminal, so I can take him to the police. Ghosts can do everything I am told.'

She stopped in her tracks and shouted, 'I am not a ghost.'

'I knew it!' Sameer slapped his thigh. 'For some crazy reason, you are trying to impersonate Arati.'

'No. I am just a lost soul—Arati's soul.'

He peered into the semi-darkness, trying to study her expression. 'If you are Arati's soul, you should help me find the culprit – it will bring your parents peace. It may also stop you from wandering. Will you lead me to him?' Sameer didn't know why he was pleading with a ghost.

'All right! I will lead you to him, if you think it will make my parents happy.' She clambered onto the pillion seat and instructed him to drive in the direction she was pointing in.

She guided Sameer through the congested parts of the city, till they reached the outskirts. 'Are you taking me to another state?' he joked, but she remained silent.

They sped through the lesser inhabited parts of the city for several kilometres until they were near the boundary of the national capital area. It was an unfamiliar territory. 'How much further?' he asked. Not a soul was around the place, and Sameer was worried he would run out of fuel.

'There he is, in the car right in front of us,' she said and pointed at a swanky red car ahead. There was a gleeful note in her voice as she said, 'As usual, he is drunk.'

Sameer tried to speed up, but the chap was going too fast.

'Stop!' Arati commanded. 'Wait here, in the shadows, as I finish this.'

She seemed to float at super-fast speed towards the car, and Sameer lost sight of her. Suddenly, he heard the screech of brakes and then a loud crash. Disobeying her instructions, he drove towards the sound.

Arati stood right in the centre of the road, blocking the path of the red car, which seemed to have skidded as the driver braked to save Arati. It skidded off the road and smashed into a large tree by the roadside before bursting into flames.

Horrified, Sameer watched the mangled car burn, aware there was no way to save the driver. He turned to look at Arati, but she had disappeared, her spirit finally having avenged her death. Shaking his head sadly, Sameer embarked on the long drive home.'

'Just goes to emphasize that even ghosts don't like to be taken for a ride,' the narrator said, ending his story, and laughing raucously.

'Bravo!' commented the lady in the black sari.

9

THE NEW YEAR PARTY

'Any more stories?' Keshavmama looked around expectantly. He seemed to be enjoying the stories as much as his guests and seemed to have no interest in ending the session.

'Me? me!' A hesitant hand went up from the other end of the table. 'I will tell you one about a murderous young man, and a victim who was bent upon taking revenge.' And so, yet another storyteller took over the thread. He cleared his throat and began, 'The executioner led him to the gallows and slipped a hood over his head. Next came the noose around his neck. Advait Saxena had seen the face of his executioner just before the hood blinded him. It was Riaan, with his half-burned face, snarling lips, and evilly bared fang-like teeth.

He begged and pleaded for mercy, but all he got was the maniacal laughter of his tormentor. The wind moaned eerily outside, and the doors rattled loudly. A blood-curdling scream rent the ominous atmosphere. And then, the noose tightened. Advait's limbs flailed and stilled. Someone was in the room throttling him. He couldn't breathe. His lungs bursting, he gasped and drew a series of sharp breaths.

He wanted to scream, but it remained buried in his throat as he continued to thrash around the bed. The air conditioner continued to hum. It was set to a low temperature, and yet he had broken into a cold sweat. He could feel the creepy presence that continued to torment him each night. It whispered a hair-raising message into his ears, sending chills down his spine. He felt asphyxiated. His heart seemed to stop, and he trembled. It was the same nightmare that had not allowed him any sleep for the past three years.

Gasping for breath, he rushed to the windows and threw them open. Then, thrusting his head out of his eleventh-floor apartment, he hungrily swallowed mouthfuls of air.

Advait had tried every method imaginable to get rid of the ghost that haunted his house. He paid enormous amounts of money to doctors, paranormal investigators, ghost hunters, and exorcists. Each of them tried to purge the spooks, but nothing worked. The ghosts remained firmly entrenched in the plush apartment. They wouldn't allow him to rest or sleep. He was a rich man, but his riches could not help him sleep.

The next morning, he called the psychoanalyst he had been consulting for the past two years. 'I can't take it anymore!' he cried. 'I haven't slept a wink for the last three years, and now I think I am on the point of a nervous breakdown.'

'I have already suggested that you undergo hypnotherapy, Mr Saxena,' said the psychoanalyst. He was the most qualified and expensive one in the city. 'Your problem is because of your repressed memories and emotions. Hypnotherapy will allow us to explore what lies underneath the rational part of your mind. We have tried other means, but your problem is very deep-seated, and it is impossible to address unless we go deeper into the brain. I see no point in continuing our sessions if you don't go to a hypnotherapist.'

'Please help me! I will do whatever you suggest.'

There was a long pause as the psychoanalyst consulted his diary. 'I can see you next week ...'

'No,' Advait cried. 'Don't you understand? I can't wait that long. I am going mad – slowly and surely. I have diabetes and heart blockages, my lungs are shrinking – I am *dying*.'

'Please, Mr Saxena, calm down. It's not good for you to be so agitated. I have no slot available this week ...'

'I beg you!' Advait interrupted. 'Please make time for me. I will pay any amount for an appointment – I am desperate.'

'In that case, I can accommodate you late evening. Can you reach my office at 9 p.m.? The hypnotherapist will be there, and together we will take you through a regression session.'

'I will be there,' promised the desperate man.

At 8.30 p.m. sharp, Advait presented himself at the psychoanalyst's office. His red-rimmed and swollen eyes looked haunted, his complexion was mottled, his body shrunken. His speech was slurred as though he had been drinking, and there was a nervous tic in his right eye. The tremors in his hands confirmed his state of extreme nervousness. The man looked like a ghost of his former self. He continued to pace the waiting room impatiently till the psychoanalyst was ready to see him.

Half an hour later, Advait entered the softly lit room that he had once admired. With its pastel green floral wallpaper, thick carpet, large window with wispy, billowing curtains and comfortable couch, it was a room designed to put a person at ease. Right from the paintings on the wall to the potted plants in the various corners of the room, each element generated an aura of peace. But it didn't work on him. Peace and calm were far from his mind.

'Please relax, Mr Saxena,' said the psychoanalyst. 'Anxiety will not help. This is my colleague, Dr Sengupta. He's one of the foremost hypnotherapists in the country – you are in good hands.'

Despite all the agitation and restlessness, a few minutes later, Advait lay stretched out on the cushioned couch. He closed his eyes and obeyed the hypnotherapist. Dr Sengupta turned out to be as good as promised and Advait felt himself relaxing. Soon, he lay hypnotized on the couch.

'I want you to go back three years and narrate the events that took place on New Year's Eve,' said the soft voice of the hypnotherapist.

From his previous sessions with Advait, the psychoanalyst had learned that a traumatic event had taken place during a

New Year's Eve party thrown in a remote location three years ago, and that had resulted in his patient's problems. But Advait Saxena had been too deeply upset to share the details of the event, evading all questions about the party. As a result, it had not been possible to cleanse his patient's mind and cure the malaise. It was time to get to the root of the problem. Without that, there would be no solution.

At first, his voice was low, and words were disjointed and garbled. The two doctors drew closer and listened carefully to the patient, who was in a trance. Gradually, the voice grew stronger, and the words became clearer.

'It was New Year's Eve, and we were at Riaan's farmhouse, the Ataraxia, partying with friends and clients,' Advait said.

'Who is Riaan?' asked Dr Sengupta.

'Riaan Mehra and I were partners at R&A Associates, a real estate business we had set up five years ago. It was Riaan's idea to catch up with friends and business partners – I thought it was a waste of money.'

Advait began to narrate the details of the conversation between Riaan and himself.

'"No, Adi, I don't consider it a waste of money. This gives us an opportunity to carry out publicity and marketing subtly. One has to do this for business," he had said when I objected to the lavish arrangements which were going to make a dent in our profits. "We'll make it up, don't you worry. Besides, we have been working too hard and we need a break."

'He brushed aside all my objections and ordered the best wine and food, of which he was a connoisseur. The only concession he made was to limit the guest list to thirty people.

'The two of us had known each other a long time. We'd gone to the same school before we went to business school. Although we were friends, we were very different people. Right from our attitude, and approach to business to our looks and personality, we were totally unlike. Riaan was handsome and popular. Girls swarmed around him. A ready smile and smooth manner made him an excellent communicator. Conversely, I wasn't good with people. People told me that the permanent scowl pasted on my face didn't encourage friendship.

'Once we had graduated from business school, we began taking things seriously. We pooled our resources to start our dream business. Real estate seemed a good idea when we set up shop, but soon the trends changed, and it hit a low phase. The competition was stiff and the deals scarce, but we persisted. It took us a couple of years of back-breaking work to re-establish ourselves. We broke even in the third year, and by the end of the fourth year, we were looking at a healthy balance sheet. The fifth year ended with a big offer which was slated to be signed in a couple of days. It was guaranteed to catapult our enterprise to a higher level.

'My talents lay in accounting and finance. I was good with figures and excellent at strategizing. Keeping our respective aptitudes in mind, we had decided that Riaan would take care of marketing and sales, while I took charge of number crunching. The arrangement worked very well for our business.

'For Riaan and me, the coming year promised all good things. The business was looking up, and we were about to sign another lucrative deal.

'Riaan believed in enjoying life. He invested most of his earnings in a farmhouse and a fancy car, while I scrimped and squirreled away money. The farmhouse was an idyllic place in a remote village far from the city. It was a recent acquisition, and the amount of money spent in doing up the place took my breath away. But then it was Riaan's money, to be spent as he pleased. The interior designer was staggeringly expensive, as was the stuff that went into it.

'My partner was a gregarious chap. Unlike me, he enjoyed partying. He lived life king-size. Money just flowed out of his pockets. His bank balance was always low, and his loan amount high. Once the farmhouse was ready, he went and bought the latest Porsche 911 – it cost a bomb! "What's the point in saving money" he would say, "when we don't know the length of our life? Besides, one can always make more money."

'Even though he was my friend, I hated Riaan. I hated him because he was so good-looking. Women, the beautiful farmhouse, and an impressive car – he had everything I wanted. That night when we gathered at the Ataraxia, I hated him even more. He was the cynosure of every eye in the hall. The women flocked around him, the men envied him. I stood in a corner, staring at the man I had secretly hated most of my life. He was everything I aspired to be.

'But what galled me the most was the manner in which he had behaved. He had treated me shabbily, often ridiculing me in gatherings, in front of others. His condescending attitude worsened with each passing day.

'The party was in full swing, the dance floor was crowded with gyrating couples. The DJ played the latest hits, the bass making hearts thump. Gorgeous women with smiles painted on their faces made small talk with men with glasses of alcohol in their hand. Loud laughter and cigarette smoke filled the hall. Everyone was eager to give the new year a thumping welcome.

'At the party, Riaan spent the entire evening circulating among the guests, refilling their glasses and making small talk, while I hung around in the background watching everyone. My eyes missed nothing. Riaan was drinking like a fish. He'd never known when to stop. I sauntered towards my friend, who was now standing with a group of women. They laughed at his silly jokes and flirted with him. Even the married ones couldn't keep away.

'Here comes Advait,' he drawled. 'He's a financial wiz, but he's also a wallflower. You won't find him on the dance floor or at the bar.'

'That can't be true!' exclaimed one of the women around him. 'Everyone gets on the dance floor during a new year bash.'

'Not Adi! He's a saint. He doesn't drink or sleep with women,' Riaan chuckled. 'He loves his calculator more than women.'

'Riaan!' I cried, trying to leash my temper.

'What? Come on, prove me wrong,' he challenged, pushing me towards a woman. 'Take her to the dance floor. Let's see you dance. But first, take a sip of whiskey. It will give you the courage to flirt,' he said, extending his glass towards me.

'Let's prove him wrong,' said the woman, smiling seductively. 'Let's dance.' She tugged at my hand. I pushed her away.

'What did I tell you? Adi doesn't dance!' Riaan said, throwing a pitying look at me.

I stormed out of the hall into the garden, my heart hammering. Standing in the garden, I plotted and planned, waiting for an opportunity to strike back at my smug friend.

I was dying to wipe that smile off his face. But it would have to wait.

It was late when the guests departed, leaving the place in a mess. Glasses were scattered around the entire house and on the outside, there were scraps of food on the floor, used plates heaped in the kitchen, and empty bottles sitting on the sofas. The entire house seemed to have been hit by a tornado.

'Let's grab some sleep before sunrise.' Riaan tottered towards the stairs, making his way towards the bedroom. 'I am dead tired.'

'You don't want to get back to town?'

'My dear friend, it's long past midnight and I am drunk. I don't want to drive back at this hour.'

'But ...'

'No, let's go to bed – we can leave later. Come on, Adi, it's New Year's Day. We have no wives waiting at home.'

'I had to attend to some work,' I scowled unhappily. 'I am not drunk, and I can drive while you sleep off the alcohol in the back seat.' I had long wanted to drive the Porsche 911.

'N ... n ... no, my dear. No one drives my car. No offence – I love you like a brother and all that, but I am possessive about my Porsche. Besides, driving through the ghats at night is not safe.'

The two of us had driven to the farmhouse together in Riaan's car. The Ataraxia was quite a distance from Mumbai, and there was no way I could get back to the city at that hour.

'Riaan, we have a very important business meeting in two days' time, and I have a hundred papers to go through before we sign on the dotted line.'

'Relax, partner. The papers can wait for a few hours.'

'Had you told me about your plans, I would have gone back with one of the guests,' I said, gritting my teeth.

'It's okay, brother. Just enjoy the place for the night. We will leave early in the morning,' Riaan said, lurching into a bedroom.

'I had had enough. My mind was made up. I would kill my partner that very night. I waited until he began to snore, and then I smothered him with a pillow. He thrashed wildly, but I continued to hold the pillow on his face for a long time till all movement ceased, and his body went limp. He was dead. I went to the bathroom, ran scalding water in the bathtub and dumped his body into it.

'I then went to the kitchen, which had a couple of gas cylinders. I cut off the hoses that connected them to the stoves and threw a lit match at the gas hissing out of the cylinders before running out of the house. Within minutes, the fire spread through the hall.

Fire! Fire!' I shouted, running towards the garage where Riaan's Porsche was parked. It was dangerous to go to the garage, but it was a chance I had to take. There was a sudden explosion before I could reach the car, and something hit my chest and I lost consciousness.

'The next morning, I woke up in the local hospital with burn injuries. The doctors told me that some locals had seen the house burning. They had alerted the others, but they couldn't do anything to save the house. They found me lying a little distance from the garage and dragged me away from the fire. It took the fire brigade a long time to bring things under control, and whatever remained of Riaan's charred body was found a few days later. The investigators found no evidence of foul play.

'I claimed to have no recollection of the accident. The doctors diagnosed it as short-term memory loss. The lack of evidence and my burned face led to the closure of the case. The investigators found nothing to indicate foul play. Riaan was an orphan who had been brought up by an uncle. The uncle had also passed away the previous year, and there were no claimants to Riaan's property. Since Riaan had no family and heirs, the business now belonged to me.

'I spent the next few weeks in a Mumbai hospital. The doctors tried their best, but there wasn't much they could do for my face, which was badly disfigured.

'Two months later, I signed the deal with a company constructing a huge office complex. It was a big deal, and I became a wealthy man.

'I did not know of the depths of my acting talents till I made a great show of mourning for my friend. In a show of magnanimity, I set up some charity trusts in my deceased partner's name and gave away a sizeable amount of money.

'A garlanded picture of Riaan continues to adorn my office. In the meantime, R&A Associates went from strength to strength. The number of our employees increased, and business flourished. But old sins have a way of sticking to a person. The horror of my deeds refused to leave me. My burned face mocked me each time I looked in the mirror, and people avoided looking at my ghastly face. But one can do a lot with money. I went abroad to undergo plastic surgery, which reconstructed my face.

'A year after the fire, I married a beautiful woman. I was living in a luxurious apartment, driving a fancy car, belonged to an exclusive club, and my business had expanded beyond imagination. I should have been happy, but the nightmares continue to haunt me. Riaan won't allow me to relax or get over my guilt. He is a constant shadow – mocking, tricking and torturing me. I can't sleep.'

Advait Saxena stopped speaking. His confession shocked the two doctors. The psychoanalyst switched off the recorder and nodded at the hypnotherapist. The two of them realized that a murderer was lying on the couch. There was just one thing to do.

The psychoanalyst stole out of the room and called the police.'

'So, what do you think of the story?' asked the narrator anxiously.

'It was a splendid story that supports my point of view,' applauded the man from the army.

With that, the field was left open for the next narrator.

10

THE SCHOLARLY SPECTRE

'Now that you have done with almost everyone, let me tell you an experience that will establish there are scholarly ghosts in the world. I am a professor and have spent several years working in universities abroad, and I have had many interesting experiences. I will now narrate one of my favourite stories,' said the bespectacled, scholarly-looking man seated to Uday's right.

A scholarly ghost sounded interesting, and Uday looked curiously at the professor.

'Hear, hear!' clamoured the guests.

'Let's hear it then!' Keshavmama rubbed his hands gleefully, and the professor began.

'Ira Mukherjee woke up with a start. The room had gone cold, and she was shivering. She noticed the window was open.

Strange! I distinctly remember shutting it last night. She was not a forgetful person and keeping warm was something she always remembered to do. Ever since she was a child, her mother had cautioned her against catching a chill because she was prone to tonsilitis. Her teeth chattering, she padded up to the window and peered out. A chilly wind blew into the room before she could shut and bolt the window.

Have I made a mistake by coming here? wondered Ira. She sat at the study table by the window and stared out at the bleak, deserted street. The icy cold weather wasn't making things better, and sunless days always dampened her mood. She was a cheerful girl who thrived in the company of friends, and she had yet to make any at Oxford.

Ira considered making a quick call home but dropped the idea. Getting a call from her at that hour would certainly alarm her parents in Kolkata. She felt homesick. It was only the fear of being ridiculed that kept her from quitting her course and returning home. Their nosey relatives would arrive promptly and drown her parents in questions. Why had she come back without completing her course? Was she in trouble? There would be much speculation, and the grapevine would buzz with gossip. She could face inquisitive folks, but her parents would find it embarrassing to explain her actions.

She had battled hard to get into Oxford. The long hours of cramming and toiling to appear for various competitive examinations had sapped her energy. But she did what it takes to attain her goal. Studying at Oxford had been her cherished dream, and she couldn't let it go.

The dream had taken shape a couple of years ago, when she visited her uncle in England, after finishing her graduation in English. She had wanted to visit him for a long time, but her studies had kept her chained to her desk. An avid reader, she had devoured scores of books set in that country, and she had secretly nursed the dream of studying there one day.

It was during that visit that Anirban Mukherjee took his niece to Oxford, which was much more beautiful than Ira had imagined. She had stared with admiration at the ancient structures that were more imposing and elegant than their descriptions. The pale Cotswold limestone buildings speckled with lichen, the latticed windows, vaulted roofs, exquisite sculptures, and lofty spires—even the most lyrical accounts of dreaming spires couldn't do the place justice. Ira craned her neck to gaze with reverence at the famous colleges that had housed some of the most eminent scholars in the world.

She had stared at the students cycling busily along the street, envying them for studying in the striking buildings. They had the privilege of poring over rare and precious tomes in the famous Bodleian Library. A scholarly air had hung around the entire place, and it seemed like a place that encouraged the exchange of ideas and fruitful debates.

By the time she returned to Kolkata, Ira's mind was made up. She wanted to pursue postgraduate studies in English literature at Oxford. She had a long discussion with her uncle, who was very supportive of the idea. What had followed was a painstaking process of collecting information, and applying for admission. Ira did not tell her parents anything till she had an acceptance letter.

Her parents, Pranab and Minoti, were aghast when she showed them the letter.

'Why don't you continue your studies in India?' asked Pranab. 'We have excellent universities here.'

'Ira, don't leave India. We need you,' pleaded Minoti. She was convinced that her daughter wouldn't return to India. No one returned. She knew of umpteen examples in their neighbourhood where the children who went abroad to study took up jobs there and refused to return to India.

Her parents were reluctant to let her go. She was their only child, and they had been planning to get her married soon.

'I am not too far away,' Ira's uncle argued. He lived in Wokingham, which was just an hour's drive from Oxford. 'What are you worried about? I will take full responsibility for Ira's well-being.'

In the end, Ira's parents had to yield to her wishes, and she winged her way to London.

Once the admission process had been completed, she settled in the room allotted to her. The room, at the end of a long passage, was equipped with a bed, wardrobe, study table, and chair. Its only window opened towards a street packed with old houses and shops. Ira unpacked and tried to create a homely atmosphere by putting up a couple of pictures. She placed the Japanese Kokeshi doll, which was a gift from her uncle and her lucky mascot, on the table along with the laptop.

For the first few days, Ira was wrapped up in her newfound freedom, and there was so much to acquaint herself with. Once the formalities were over, her studies started in earnest. She was thankful for the anonymity the place offered. There were no nosy characters to pry into her life.

Ira was doing well and gradually, the pace of her studies picked up and she had to work late into the night to be well prepared for the next day. She rarely joined her classmates who were bent on having a good time, going out every day after classes to shop or for a meal. She was determined to be on top of the class, and that required hard work. And so, a month glided away swiftly.

Everything was going well till, one night, the sound of scraping woke Ira up. Her chair, which faced the window, was pulled to a side. To her annoyance, her things on the table were scattered around messily.

Ira was a meticulous person and a cleanliness freak. She liked her things to be placed in a certain order and had maintained the same order forever. So orderly was her room that she could locate whatever she wanted even if she were to walk around blindfolded. Her compulsive neatness was a joke in the family.

She was going back to sleep when she noticed that her laptop, which she had switched off, had suddenly come to life. Ira noticed that the assignment on which she had been working was now open on the screen. To her horror, she saw the text she had been keying into the page being deleted slowly. It was as though someone was pressing the backspace key. Letter by letter, word by word, line by line, the entire text of her assignment was being deleted. One page and then another, the strange phenomenon went on.

Something incredibly bizarre was taking place right in front of her eyes. She was too stunned to react for a few minutes. Then, with a loud exclamation, she switched on the light and ran towards her desk. She tapped the backspace key a few times to make sure that it was not stuck. All her efforts to stop the key from obliterating her work failed. It simply refused to obey her. Desperate, she tried to shut the machine but failed. What was happening? Was her machine malfunctioning? The backspace key must have got jammed, though it did not appear so. What a nuisance! She had lost an entire day's work.

Her mind was spinning, and it was impossible to go back to sleep. Ira tossed and turned for the rest of the night. She would have to get the laptop repaired or buy a new one, and that was just one part of the problem – reworking the project was a bigger part. She had spent hours in the library finding that material and then worked long hours to complete the assignment. And now it was all gone.

There was a fresh surprise waiting for her in the morning. The backspace key was now working perfectly fine, and the laptop seemed to have no problem. Ira could find no explanation for her assignment being deleted the previous night. Sighing exasperatedly, she went to work once again. This time, it took longer to finish the project because she couldn't concentrate on her work. Despite all attempts, her mind continued to fly back to the strange happenings the previous night, and a headache threatened to ruin her day.

She worked late into the night to finish the assignment. This time, she saved a copy in another location just in case.

She ensured the window was latched and arranged her things the way she liked before hitting the sack. Exhausted after the day's work, she fell asleep almost immediately.

Barely an hour later, she was woken up by a chill in the room. Ira pulled the duvet tighter around her and burrowed under it, but she was still shivering. *Isn't the radiator working*? she wondered.

Cursing, she sat up and stared at the window. It was open.

It was like the nightmare was repeating itself. Just like the previous night, her things were scattered across the study table. The laptop was switched on, and she noticed that her assignment was being deleted again. Enraged, she sprung out of bed and rushed to tap the backspace button. And just like the previous night, it refused to comply. Word by word, para by para, her work disappeared again. Ira shut the window and collapsed on the bed, sobbing.

The next morning, her laptop was working perfectly – *again*. Was it someone playing a prank on her? Why couldn't she see the person? Was it being deleted through some kind of remote device? Had it been hacked? It defied all logic.

Ira decided to keep watch the next night. She wanted to confront the culprit and demand an explanation. Armed with a flask of coffee, she had the lights switched on as she sat on the bed, reading a book.

Precisely at midnight, just as the church bells announced the hour, the window flew open. An icy breeze invaded the room, and she shivered. Invisible hands upset the pen stand on the table and pushed things about randomly. Then, the nightmare began. The laptop screen lit up, and she watched as her assignment was opened up and the backspace button was pressed down. Like before, words began disappearing as an invisible hand systematically deleted the assignment. Ira trembled. Her legs were like jelly. She couldn't stand or do anything. Shocked, she continued to watch the eerie happenings unfold in the room. She felt faint.

No, I won't be weak. I have to fight back against this unfair treatment. I have done no wrong. Steeling herself, she cleared her throat.

'Who are you?' she shouted. 'Why are you doing this to me? I have harmed no one.'

There was no response to her questions. The phantom fingers continued to work silently on her project. The words continued to be deleted even as she watched helplessly. And just like that, the work that had taken her many hours to finish vanished. Once the entire project had vanished, the laptop was shut down. It was the third time she had worked on the same assignment.

It can't be a human. Could it be a spirit? Ira wondered, tossing restlessly on her bed. It was impossible to sleep.

The next morning, she was convinced that there was a ghost in her room. Some frustrated student who could not tolerate her excellent grades. She wouldn't work on that project, Ira decided. She couldn't bear to spend hours on it only to find it being deleted.

She abandoned that assignment and worked on another one. To her horror, the process repeated itself. Each time she completed an assignment, a new one or something she was redoing, invisible fingers deleted it word for word from her laptop. Even the backup copies she saved vanished from the system.

That night, Ira left a message on the table.

Dear invisible one,

I do not know who you are or what your purpose is. All I know is that I am here to study, and you are getting in my way. What can I do to help you so that you let me live in peace?

A much-troubled soul,
Ira

Ira cracked her knuckles impatiently as she waited for a response.

Suddenly, fresh words began appearing magically on the screen as someone tapped the keys rapidly.

Dear Troubled Soul,

I would be delighted if you could help me. I promise to leave you in peace once my work is over.

Spectre

Making her way to her desk, Ira typed out,

What's your work? Surely it can't be achieved by deleting my work.

Within seconds came an answer.

I want you to edit my manuscript and get it published. My soul will be at peace once that happens. In return, I promise to help you finish all your assignments.

The strange demand horrified Ira, and her fingers flew over the keyboard again as she wrote,

I barely have time to finish my assignments. How can I edit your manuscript?

Also, I don't know who you are. Your name can't be 'Spectre.' The least you can do is give me the correct information.

Ten seconds later, words began to appear on the screen.

My name is James Harrington. Just like you, I studied English literature and nursed dreams of becoming a famous author. I lived in this room for two years, working hard to keep up with my classes while working on my novel. My grades were good, and the manuscript was shaping up very well. I sent my manuscript to several publishers, but all I received were rejections.

Invisible hands continued to fly over the buttons, and words filled the screen.

You can't imagine my frustration. The rejections shattered my self-confidence. No matter how many times I edited and reworked the novel, the manuscript just wasn't being accepted by any publisher. I slowly sank into a depression. Finally, unable to bear the humiliation, I hung myself.

Ira's skin tingled and goosebumps covered her arms. Her hand flew to her mouth as she gasped. The ghost had once lived in this very room. He had a name, and he was real. Touched by the story, she typed,

What do you want me to do?

Immediately came a reply.

I already told you. I want you to edit my manuscript and get it published.

Making a face, Ira typed out an objection.

I will edit your manuscript, but I can't ensure it gets published.

James responded by saying,

One step at a time. It has been a tedious task, but I have managed to type my manuscript on your laptop. Start editing it, and then we will see. I know that stories similar to mine are back in demand.

For a few minutes, Ira sat stunned before her laptop. Then, she began hunting for James's manuscript. It was there, running to 85,000 words, in a folder on Ira's laptop. Her heart hammering, she opened the document and began reading. It was an exciting story set against the background of the Second World War. The only real issue Ira found was the dated language. All she had to do was rewrite the entire manuscript to make it read like a contemporary work.

She decided to complete the editing as soon as possible so that she could get back to her lessons. Ira devoted three to four hours every night to the manuscript. In the day, she attended classes and worked on her projects, and by night, she was back to working on the manuscript. In the meantime, James kept his word by working on her projects, and he was good at it too.

Three full months of hard work later, Ira had finished rewriting James' novel. The lack of sleep had given her dark circles, and she looked exhausted. But the manuscript read much better – she felt satisfied, and James was excited.

You are a gem, he typed one evening. *You will not regret this, I promise.*

She sent the manuscript to several agents and received a positive response from one. The agent, a well-known one at that, had liked the story and was willing to take it to various publishers. To her utter delight, he soon found a publisher, who then wanted to know the name of the author.

Ira discussed it with an ecstatic James. She could almost see him jumping around with joy.

The publishers want to use your actual name. Spectre isn't a good pseudonym they feel, Ira's fingers tapped out on her keyboard.

No, they have to use the pseudonym, James insisted. *That's what I am—a spectre. You will be my voice.*

In the end, the publishers agreed to use the pseudonym.

It was spring by the time the novel was published. At James' insistence, it was launched by Ira at his favourite café.

'I am just a messenger, carrying out instructions,' she said to the large gathering of curious students. The author's name had drawn them to the event, and the publishers had spent a reasonable amount of money for publicity. Among the invitees were several newspaper and magazine reporters. 'The author wanted it to go under that name,' she replied when asked about who had authored the book and what was the author's "actual name".

'But why "Spectre"?' asked a reporter. 'Is there a spooky element in the book?'

'You are absolutely right,' said Ira. 'The book has been written by a ghost.'

Disbelief and laughter rang through the audience, as the people thought Ira was joking. Most of them had assumed she was the author.

'Where is Spectre?' demanded a student. 'We want to meet the author.'

It was time then for Ira to narrate the story. She shared the story of a young man's dream and the frustration that followed his hard work. She provided a blow-by-blow account of how a book that had been written more than fifty years ago was edited and brought up to date.

No one believed the story, but the book was a bestseller. The story was published in newspapers and magazines. Soon, everyone wanted to read the book written by a ghost. The newspaper reporters, keen to learn the truth of Ira's story, pored through police and university records. It was verified that a twenty-two-year-old student called James Harrington had hung himself in Ira's room. Once the story was printed in the newspapers, several people came forward claiming to have heard of James Harrington. Some of them were genuine, too.

The publisher wanted Ira to go on a book tour through Europe. It was a whirlwind of activities as she travelled from one city to another, talking about her encounter with James and her experiences.

The success of the book made Ira feel heady and she basked in the limelight. Could this be happening? What had started as a frightening and unearthly experience, now felt like an adventure. It took a while for her excitement to calm. There were more practical matters to deal with.

What should I do with the royalties? Ira asked James. Royalty cheques had begun arriving at Anirban's address, which she had given to the publishers.

Set up a trust for students who aspire to be writers. Each year, we will fund the most promising person and provide a scholarship so they can devote their time to writing. James' instructions were clear.

Get up, lazy bum. Ira heard a voice, early one morning. Sitting up with a start, she rubbed her eyes and looked around the room. There was no one. It was still dark and misty outside. *It's me. James.*

Am I going mad? Ira wondered. I am hearing his voice now. This has to end. *What do you want, now?* She asked, irritated.

Just get up. You won't regret it, I promise. Ira heard him say.

It's very early, James, and I am so exhausted.

We are going somewhere. I want you to see something! His voice was moody.

Where? At this godforsaken hour? Have a heart, James! Besides, how am I to follow you when I don't even know what you look like?

Just do as I say, he insisted. *This might be the last thing I ask you to do for me. All you have to do is to follow my shadow. Don't worry, only you will be able to see the shadow.*

I hope whatever you have planned is worth the trouble.

Oh, absolutely! As I said, you won't regret it one bit.

Wondering where this was going, Ira got dressed. Soon, she saw a shadow falling across her door. Grumbling, she followed the shadow down the road. Dawn's paintbrush had streaked the sky, gold and pink, and a new day had arrived. It was still early, but the city was stirring, and early morning joggers dotted the streets.

They walked past Merton College, then the Pembroke and Exeter colleges. James appeared excited. His shadow skipped quickly ahead and she followed. Leaving JRR Tolkien's house behind, they continued walking towards the Wolvercote Cemetery.

'Why are we here?' Ira panted out the question. She was tired.

This is where JRR Tolkien is buried. The shadow seemed to speak as they passed a modest, open grave with a tombstone that confirmed that Edith Mary Tolkien and John Ronald Reuel Tolkien were buried there.

'I know – I've been here before!' Ira said in exasperation. She had gone on a tour of the entire place a couple of days after arriving at Oxford. James had dragged her out of her bed at an unearthly hour and made her walk all this distance just to show her where Tolkien was buried? 'We could have come at any other time. Why so early and why on foot?' she shouted.

Patience, my dear! James chuckled as he continued to lead her around the gravestones till they reached a small one at one corner of the cemetery. *There's a method to my madness.*

James finally halted at a grave. *Read the text on the tombstone, he said in a shaky voice.*

James Mathew Harrington
18 April 1921 – 8 September 1943
No farewell words were spoken,
No time to say goodbye,
You were gone before we knew it,
and only God knows why.

'This is where you are buried,' Ira whispered.

Yes, Ira. My restless soul has wandered too many years, but now I am at peace. Thanks to your efforts, I no longer have to haunt the halls like so many others who still haunt Oxford. Farewell, my dear – bless you!

The next instant, there was a whirl of smoke and a light seemed to glow for a moment over the grave, and then it was all quiet. Ira realized James was now finally at rest six feet underground. She was finally rid of the ghost, but the realisation didn't bring her happiness.

That evening, Ira returned to the cemetery with a bunch of yellow lilies and a copy of James' book. She cleaned the tomb and placed the book and flowers on it. *I'll miss you*, she whispered. In the last few months, James had become a part of her life.'

The professor ended his story.

'Well, I'll be damned!' commented the soldier. 'That girl was rather spunky, I must say. Imagine living with a ghost for so many months.'

'But it was a friendly ghost,' the anthropologist remarked.

It was the final speaker's turn, and everyone turned to her in anticipation. 'The spook in my story is not a friendly one. In fact, it's a rather strange story of rebirth. As a psychologist, I have come across some cases that defy the imagination.'

'Oh, do begin,' pleaded a reedy voice. 'It's sure to be interesting.'

11

THE STRANGE STORY OF RISHABH MISHRA

'Prashant Mishra stood with his son, Rishabh, a lad of eight, outside the elegant double-storied house and looked around. The plush house stood amid a beautifully landscaped garden. The latest Audi graced the porch.

'This is my house,' said Rishabh, his eyes running around the place. 'Nothing has changed – except the car. I drove a Skoda.'

'Pshhh! No more of this talk, Rish. Remember what I said. We are here to verify some things, not to blame anyone or take any action. Let me do the talking – you will not utter a single word,' warned Prashant.

He hesitated for a moment, trying to marshal his thoughts and frame his sentences, and then pressed the doorbell. He heard the bell ring inside the house, and a dog begin to bark. It was several minutes before the door opened, and a young man stood there, looking curiously at the visitors.

'Yes?' he said. 'May I help you?'

Rishabh's eager voice piped up before Prashant could respond. 'We're here to meet Sunil Mehta. Is he at home?'

An expression of sadness appeared momentarily on the young man's face. 'My brother died in a road accident several years ago,' he said, frowning at the visitors. The child was staring at him strangely, as though he could read his mind, and it made him uncomfortable. 'Is there anything I can do for you?'

'So, you're still here, Dev?' Rishabh asked.

'How do you know my name?' asked the young man, looking surprised. 'I don't think we've met.'

'I know your name and everything about you. You're Devansh, Sunil's first cousin.'

Prashant nudged his son, reminding him to be silent, and took over the conversation. 'Thanks, Devansh. We wanted to meet Sunil.' He began pulling his son back, but Rishabh was unwilling to give up.

'Is Priya home?' he asked.

Devansh looked flabbergasted. The boy seemed to know her. 'You want to meet Priya?' he asked, wondering what the child wanted. 'Look, I don't know who you are and why you want to meet Sunil or Priya. Sunil is dead, and Priya is busy. It's not a convenient time for us to entertain visitors. Why don't you visit the office after an hour?'

'But we have come all the way from Delhi to meet her ...' Rishabh protested.

'It's all right!' Prashant interrupted his son. 'Thank you for your time. We'll visit her at the office.'

'Who is it, darling?' said a beautiful woman, suddenly appearing at the door. 'I heard you speaking to someone.' She stared at Devansh, who looked shaken. 'Is there a problem?'

'Nothing, darling!' said Devansh. 'These people wanted to meet Sunil, and they're asking for you. I have told them to meet us at the office after an hour.'

'Why do they want to meet Sunil?' She narrowed her eyes suspiciously as she looked at the two of them.

Rishabh stared back at the woman and said, 'I have a reason.'

Before he could say anything else, Prashant tugged at his son's hand. 'Let's go,' he said. 'We will see them later.'

A dog shot out of the house just as they neared the gate. Instead of barking at the visitors, it began whining and licking the child's hand.

'Pluto, my pet, look at how big you are!' Rishabh said, hugging the Labrador. 'Do you miss me?'

'Pluto! Get inside,' shouted the woman, still standing at the door. Pluto was behaving uncharacteristically – he wasn't friendly with strangers. 'Get inside this moment,' she ordered.

To Prashant's surprise, the dog remained rooted to the spot and continued whining as they stepped out and shut the gate behind them.

'Take us to the police station,' Prashant ordered the cab driver waiting outside. Turning to his son, he said, 'Didn't I tell you to leave the talking to me? Why did you have to speak?'

'I couldn't help myself,' Rishabh countered. 'You didn't believe me when I told you that Dev is my first cousin, and Priya is my wife. Together, they planned to get rid of me so they could marry and enjoy the fruits of my labour. Are you finally convinced that I told the truth?'

'I believe you, son,' Prashant reassured him. 'However, I want you to keep quiet when we are at the police station. I don't want you to interrupt when I speak to the police officer.'

Prashant had requested a close friend, who was a senior police officer in New Delhi, to give the name and contact of a colleague in Pune. Armed with those details, he entered the Khadki Police Station. The senior inspector, Sreekant Godbole, turned out to be a friendly person.

'What can I do for you, sir?' he asked.

'I want to know the details of an accident that took place seven years ago when a person named Sunil Mehta died.'

'Is there a specific reason for you to seek this information? The accident took place several years back, and the file is closed,' said Inspector Godbole. 'But tell me – it must be something important for you to come all the way from Delhi.'

'I have a sound reason, but it's personal,' replied Prashant. He was reluctant to share any details with the inspector.

'I can't recall the details offhand – let me ask for the file,' said Godbole shrugging. He called for the file. In his long years of service, he had come across many unusual requests, and this one did not surprise him. 'May I offer you tea while we wait?'

'No, thank you. A glass of water would be good though,' said Prashant.

The inspector busied himself with other work while they waited. 'You are right!' said Godbole after the file arrived. 'Sunil Mehta died in a car crash seven years ago.'

'Can you give me any more details?'

'I don't know too much about them, but my colleague, Parab would know,' Godbole said and called for the constable.

Fortunately for Prashant, Parab knew quite a lot about the Mehtas.

'The Mehta family is well known in this area. The senior Mehta was a builder of repute, and besides the construction business, he owned a multiplex and shopping mall. He had two sons. While Sunil, the elder one, was the responsible kind, the younger stepson was a total contrast. Irresponsible and a spendthrift, Devansh was a total disappointment to the family. In time, Sunil Mehta, the elder son, inherited the properties,' said Inspector Godbole. 'With his sharp business acumen, he expanded the business and multiplied profits many times. A handsome young man, he was one of the most eligible bachelors in town, and Sunil loved fast cars. His problems began after he fell in love and married Priya Parulkar, a woman with lofty ambitions,' Parab told them.

'Where did the accident take place?' Prashant asked.

'Sunil drove a customized Skoda. The day he died, he had gone to Mumbai on business. Priya and Devansh had also gone with him, but they stayed back for a day in Mumbai to do some shopping. Sunil had to return because of an important meeting in Pune. It was raining heavily as he drove back to Pune late that night. While manoeuvring a sharp bend, he lost control of the car, and it went down the gorge. He died instantaneously. Later, it emerged that Sunil had attended a party that evening and had had a couple of drinks. Perhaps he was too drunk to drive? We don't know.'

'Who is Devansh?'

'Devansh is Sunil's stepbrother, a wastrel. He lived in the Mehta house and depended on Sunil's generosity. Everyone was surprised when he married Priya soon after Sunil's death.' Parab's mouth twisted in distaste.

'It must have been the money. Priya must have inherited all the properties and wealth, a windfall for both Devansh and Priya,' Prashant surmised.

'That's right. She's now one of the wealthiest women in town.' The inspector toyed with his pen. He was thoughtful for a few moments and then he asked, 'I know you said it was a personal matter, but I am curious about your interest in this case.'

'You may not believe the reason that's compelled me to come all the way – it's an incredible story,' Prashant sighed as he got up to leave. 'My son, Rishabh, is eight years old. He claims he is Sunil Mehta. Thank you for all your help.'

Leaving the inspector gaping, Prashant walked out with his son.

'Take us back to the house in Range Hills,' he ordered the waiting cab driver. This time, he decided, he would allow Rishabh to speak to Devansh and Priya. That might help to get the beliefs out of the child's mind.

His mind was in a whirl as they drove to the Mehta home. So Rishabh seemed to have been right all along, he mused. Not only had he remembered the address and names of the Mehtas, he had also provided the correct details of his previous life as Sunil Mehta.

It had all started when Prashant had taken Rishabh to a kindergarten school for admission.

'What is your name?' the teacher interviewing the child had asked.

'My name is Sunil, but I am now called Rishabh,' the three-year-old had replied.

'And where do you live?'

'12, Birdwood Road, Range Hills, Pune.'

His son's replies surprised Prashant. Rishabh was an intelligent boy, but very mischievous. His replies pretty much depended on his mood. 'Don't play the fool, Rishabh! You know our address – we live in New Delhi,' he chided.

'Yes, I know we live in Delhi. But I lived in Pune for over thirty years before I started living here.'

'I am sorry, madam,' Prashant apologized. He was keen on getting his son admitted to the school, but he feared that the teacher would now reject the child. 'Rishabh is a naughty boy. He knows all the answers, I assure you.'

The teacher was an old hand and had encountered many mischievous children. She smiled indulgently at Rishabh. 'I am sure your son is a very intelligent child. He's confident, and fluent in his expressions, and that's all that matters. This is the age for mischief, and that's how it should be. We would be happy to have Rishabh here,' she said.

Prashant heaved a sigh of relief, but he could not stop himself from dressing down his son on the drive home. 'You should not tell lies, Rish.'

'I don't lie – it's the truth,' insisted his son. 'I lived in Pune, and my name was Sunil Mehta at that time.'

There was no point in arguing with the child. Rishabh was far too sharp for his age. He had suffered badly from nightmares as a child, and so his parents had been careful not to put any pressure on him. The problem was that he had a very imaginative mind and was fond of telling stories. He'd told his friends about his luxurious house and car in Pune. It was from Rishabh's friend's father that Prashant had found out about the stories that Rishabh had been telling his friends. At first, Prashant ignored the stories, but after the interview, he felt they had to discuss the matter with Rishabh.

He would ask Neelam to speak to Rishabh, Prashant decided. She had a better way of handling things and understood the whims of their son.

That night, Prashant narrated the episode at the school to his wife. 'Why don't you have a word with him?' he said. 'He will soon attend school, and such lies will create trouble.'

Neelam brushed him off, saying that Rishabh was an intelligent boy and that boys his age indulged in fanciful stories. 'He'll get over it,' she consoled her husband.

But Rishabh continued telling stories about his life as Sunil Mehta, and word travelled back to his parents. While Neelam took it in her stride, Prashant could not come to terms with his son's overactive imagination.

'Are you mad?' Prashant shouted one evening. He was returning from work when a neighbour stopped him to narrate what Rishabh had been telling their son. 'I believe that you have been telling your friends that you are married to a woman called Priya.'

'Well, it's true. I am not telling lies,' said Rishabh, defending his story.

'And may I know where she lives?'

'At my house.'

'And where is that?'

'It's in Range Hills in Pune – I've told you this before.'

'Not that story again!' Prashant was now irritated by Rishabh's stories. The boy had an answer to every question, and they would carry on arguing with no end in sight. This was not the first time this was happening. 'Enough!' Prashant shouted and left the room.

By this time, Prashant was convinced that there was something strange, surreal, about these stories.

It was a Sunday, and Prashant was cleaning the car in the garage when Rishabh came running and asked, 'Can I drive the car?'

'Sure! When you are eighteen years old, I will teach you how to drive.'

'But I know how to drive – I love driving!'

Prashant was taken aback. *This must be another of his lies*, he thought. It was time to test Rishabh's story.

Casting him a sideways glance, he said, 'Okay son, let's see you drive.'

Rishabh was terribly excited as this was the first time he would drive his dad's car. Tall for his age, the boy's feet just about reached the pedals. Prashant adjusted Rishabh's seat and sat in the passenger's seat.

The boy turned on the ignition and started the car with complete confidence, seeming perfectly at ease in the vehicle. Prashant gripped the hand brake tightly, ready to use it as the car began to move. To his surprise, the child drove slowly out of the gate, executing a neat left turn, and then smoothly changed gears. Soon, the car gathered speed.

Prashant released the hand brake. He had not expected his son to drive so smoothly – the boy drove like an expert! They drove around for about twenty minutes, after which Rishabh headed home. There was no doubt in his mind – the boy was a skilful driver.

Time flew, but Rishabh continued to insist he was Sunil Mehta. Contrary to Neelam's belief , the boy hadn't gotten over his story.

'It's time we did something about the matter, Prashant told his wife. He's eight and nothing has changed. I think we should consult a child psychologist, otherwise, he may develop complexes.'

This time, Neelam didn't object.

The very next day, the couple consulted Dr Sandip Basu, a renowned child psychologist.

'The phenomenon of recalling a past life is not very common, but it exists,' said the elderly specialist after hearing the entire story. 'It usually occurs in children between the age of five and seven. There are umpteen cases all over the world, where some children have recalled incidents from a previous life.'

'Is there something we can do?' Neelam asked. Although she had discarded Rishabh's stories as a figment of his imagination, she wondered if it could cause any long-term harm to her son.

'Why don't you bring Rishabh here?' asked Dr Basu. 'I'll have a word with him and then we can decide on a course of action.'

Two days later, the anxious parents took their son to Dr Basu, who knew his job. He soon put the boy at ease, and they got talking about school, classmates, close friends, and teachers. It didn't take long for Rishabh to narrate his story to the friendly old man who had given him chocolates and cold drinks.

'I find nothing wrong with your son,' Dr Basu reassured the parents after a few sessions. 'There is no doubt that he's experiencing the resurfacing of past life memories.'

'What can we do to help him?' Prashant wanted to know. 'I want him to have a carefree childhood, not one haunted by past fears.'

'Most children get over the recall process after a certain age. Just help him grow up normally and ignore the stories about his past life. Such memories tend to fade away with time. By the time such children reach adolescence, all memories of their past lives fade away completely,' Dr Basu advised.

'Rishabh lives in the past, Doctor. He does not seem to belong in the present,' Prashant told Dr Basu.

'Don't worry, time will heal everything.'

'Is there no cure for this?'

'Past-life regression practitioners use hypnosis and suggestions to treat such cases, but recent studies have discredited such methods. Go home and relax, and all will be fine with time. There is no need to worry.'

Neelam returned home, reassured that Rishabh would gradually forget his past life. But her husband couldn't get over his son's stories. A dozen questions troubled Prashant. Was

Rishabh telling the truth? Had he actually lived in Range Hills in Pune? Had Priya and Devansh really conspired to kill Sunil? Had they tampered with the brakes of his car? He decided to verify the authenticity of his son's story.

The next day, he bought two tickets to Pune. Once they'd landed, they'd been to Sunil's home in Range Hills, and Inspector Godbole had confirmed that Sunil Mehta had died in a car crash seven years ago. All they had to do now was confirm if Priya and Devansh had conspired to cause the accident.

There was a determined look on Prashant's face as they drove back to the Range Hills after meeting the police officer, and he rang the doorbell of the house once again.

'Go ahead and say everything you want,' he told Rishabh. 'I want you to get it out of your system—once and for all. And then, we leave for Delhi.'

The door opened, and Devansh stood staring at them. It irritated him to see the boy standing at the door.

'You?' he shouted. 'Didn't I tell you to meet us in the office? I forbid you to enter this house. Get out!'

'This is my house, and I don't need your permission to enter this house,' said Rishabh with a mature look in his eyes. His voice had changed, and he suddenly sounded like a grown man. 'Don't you recognize me? It's me, your elder brother – well, stepbrother to be more precise.'

'What rubbish!' exclaimed the furious Devansh. 'Get out before I call the police.'

'That'll be a foolish thing to do, Dev. Because then, I will be forced to tell them how Priya and you conspired to kill me to grab my property.'

There was a stunned silence as the boy and the man stared at each other.

'Don't be ridiculous,' said Devansh, looking distinctly uncomfortable. 'My brother died in a road accident several years ago.'

'Yes, he died exactly eight years and ten months ago,' replied the boy.

'Who's it, Dev?' asked a woman's voice.

'These fellows are back again,' Devansh said to Priya, who had joined them at the door. 'This *boy* claims he is Sunil.'

'*What*?' she said, breaking into loud laughter. 'Is this some kind of joke?'

'It's not a joke, Priya,' Rishabh's voice rose over her laughter. 'I am your husband, Sunil. The one you conspired to kill.'

'What nonsense! Are you crazy?' she shouted as Devansh held her hand tightly in his own.

'All right, if you are Sunil, then you must certainly know my birthdate,' said Devansh in an unsteady voice.

'It's 1 September 1988,' Rishabh said, rattling off the date in a trice.

The reply didn't convince Devansh. 'It isn't difficult to know someone's birthdate,' he scoffed.

'It is you who asked me for that information,' Rishabh replied calmly. 'You can ask me anything you want.'

'Can you narrate one incidence which no one else knows?'

'Do you remember our neighbour, Kirpal Singh, who was a collector of antiques? Kirpal Singh's son was our classmate and we often went over to his house to play. I smelt trouble when I saw you staring at a vintage pocket watch in the glass cabinet where he displayed his collection. Even at that age, you had been a covetous boy. You took the opportunity when we were invited to his son's birthday party. Sure enough, you stole the watch and a few days later, I found it hidden under your mattress. I threatened to tell everyone about your misdeed unless you returned the watch to the rightful owner. Although enraged, you kept your promise, and I didn't tell anyone about the incident.'

Devansh began to tremble. He stared at Priya for comfort, but her face had turned ashen. 'The two of you killed me,' said Rishabh.

'This isn't true!' whispered Priya.

'It's absolutely true. Despite everything I did, the two of you were not satisfied. Your greed grew, and you wanted to grab all the property,' Rishabh said, his voice sharp with anger. Pluto, who had now rushed out, lay whining at his feet. 'Pluto knows who I am. After all, a dog is more faithful than humans.'

Prashant tried to restrain his son, who was waving his hands in an agitated manner. It had been a mistake to come to Pune. He should have heeded Dr Basu's advice and let time do the healing.

'You tampered with the brakes of my car and made excuses not to return with me that night,' Rishabh raged. 'Driving through the ghats with their treacherous bends during the monsoons is a tricky affair. It offered you the perfect opportunity to get rid of me. Devansh loosened the wheel bolts and tampered with the brake wires so I could not control the car. As expected, the car's front right wheel locked when I used the emergency brake, and the car hurtled down the gorge.'

'What do you want?' Devansh asked shakily. He had been close to his stepbrother until he had fallen in love with Priya.

She had goaded him into tampering with the brakes of Sunil's car. 'We will share the wealth with you,' he now offered.

'I don't want your wealth,' Rishabh retorted. 'You are despicable, and this wealth will not bring you any happiness. You will live with this guilt all your lives. All I want is Pluto.'

'Forgive me, Sunil! My guilt has not allowed me to rest or sleep for the past seven years. Having your forgiveness will put my mind at rest,' Devansh begged.

'I will not forgive you – ever,' stormed Rishabh. 'You deserve this punishment. Be thankful that I have not lodged a police complaint against the two of you. Send Pluto to this address,' Rishabh dictated the Delhi address to the grovelling man.

'Please, Sunil ... I beg you ...' Devansh said, falling at the boy's feet.

'Nothing you say will make me forgive you and Priya.' There was a finality in his voice as Rishabh turned on his heel and tugged at Prashant's hand. 'Let's go home, Papa,' he said tiredly. 'I have got it out of my system – I am ready to be Rishabh Mishra.'

Relieved, Prashant led his son out of the bungalow.'

'Are you the psychologist in the story?' asked the army officer eagerly. 'I could use the help of one right now.'

'Dr Basu is a colleague,' the lady responded. 'I have worked with him for many years. Together, we have handled many strange cases, and this is just one of them.'

'Damn!' the officer swore. 'And I thought only the military offers an interesting life.'

Loud laughter rang across the table as everyone enjoyed the joke.

12

THE REVELATION

The last guest ended his story, and Uday heaved a sigh of relief. They could proceed with the meal at last. But suddenly, strange crackling sounds drowned the loud applause for the storyteller, and a wave of heat rose through the room.

Everyone stiffened. Suddenly, someone shouted, 'Fire! Fire!'

There was a crashing sound, and the acrid odour of burning wood irritated Uday's nostrils. A choking column of smoke poured into the room, and everyone began to cough. The enormous chandelier overhead fell to the floor with a loud crash, shattering into a thousand pieces. The earth seemed to move under them as the dining table collapsed along with the food on it. Chairs were pushed back, and people scrambled in all directions.

'Run! Get outside the house!' came the command from another guest. There was pandemonium as everyone made for the door. First, the curtains, then the upholstery, and then every inflammable item began to catch fire. The doors rattled, the crockery shattered, and the walls crumbled. Soon, the entire structure was engulfed by fire. Huge flames began licking through the roof of the house.

There was much jostling as everyone ran helter-skelter. A wall collapsed into a pile of bricks, raising a cloud of dust. His eyes watering, Uday stumbled out of the hall. He felt the earth quiver under his trembling feet. A large brick fell on his head, and he collapsed onto a pile of rubble, losing consciousness.

When he opened his eyes, the sun was shining brightly. Shocked, he looked around and found himself sitting on a pile of rubble. His bag lay at his feet. What had happened last night? Did the house collapse because of the fire? Why hadn't the firefighters arrived? Where had Keshavmama, Bhurakaka, and the guests disappeared? Were they all dead? He shivered suddenly. They *couldn't* all be dead. Who had saved him then?

Dazed, he got to his feet and staggered towards the outhouse that was home to the night watchman. But there was not a soul around. Confused, he walked out of the unhinged gate. He had walked for more than a kilometre and reached the spot where the cab had dropped him when he spotted a goatherd.

'Can you tell me if there was a fire at Shantikunj, last night?' he asked. 'Where's everyone?'

The goatherd looked alarmed. Leaving his herd behind, the man took to his heels, shouting, '*Bhoot*!'

Uday couldn't believe that the man had called *him* a ghost. He continued to wander till he reached a cluster of huts. People looked frightened and ran away when he wanted to know about Shantikunj.

'Don't you know, Babu?' asked an old man, finally answering him. 'A massive fire razed Shantikunj to the ground about six months ago.'

Stunned, Uday slumped to the ground.

'Keshav Babu was a good man. He had always campaigned against the illegal chopping of trees in this area, but there are a few timber smugglers operating in these forests. They had been getting away due to their connections,' the old man sighed. 'But things changed after Keshav Babu lodged a complaint at the police headquarters and used his influence to have them arrested. The mafia doesn't spare anyone who crosses their path. While Keshav Babu and his guests were celebrating his birthday at Shantikunj, the gang locked everyone inside and set fire to the house.'

'Didn't anyone survive?' Uday's jaw dropped in disbelief as he listened to the man.

'No, Babu. The thieves had bribed the cook to add a sedative to the food, and the people inside the house were unconscious after eating. It took some time for the locals to notice the blaze and report the fire to the nearest fire station, which is quite far. By the time the fire engines arrived, the house had turned into rubble. Keshav Babu, his guests and the servants were all trapped in the blazing house. Everyone died.'

Uday inhaled sharply as he digested the tragic news. His disbelief was quickly followed by grief, and his heart sank with despair. Shantikunj, which held innumerable happy memories, was gone forever, as was his favourite uncle. Hugging his knees close to his body, he allowed the tears to flow.

'No one goes to Shantikunj now,' whispered the old man, moved by the young man's grief. 'It's haunted by the spirits of those who died in the fire. People have seen them enjoying themselves in the large dining hall on moonless nights, just like they were on the day they died.'

It had been an incredible night. Uday's head reeled as he recalled the gathering and the eerie atmosphere in the dining hall as the guests narrated their disturbing stories.

Keshavmama, Bhurakaka, and the eleven guests. Were they a figment of his imagination? Did his feverish brain conjure up the paranormal experience? Was he hallucinating? Uday wondered.

About the Authors

Born in New Delhi, **Tanushree** worked in the corporate sector for eight long years before she quit the rat race to write.

A well-known travel writer and novelist, she is passionate about travelling and writing. Climate change and the environment are of special interest to her. Tanushree enjoys writing in various genres. This has led to her writing in historical, military, crime, and paranormal genres for adults and children.

She has written many non-fiction books before moving to fiction and has published 15 novels. Among her books are *Nurjahan's Daughter, Boots Belts Berets, On the Double, Escape from Harem, Solo in Singapore, A Closetful of Skeletons, Before you Breathe, No Margin for Error, The Teenage Diary of Rani Laxmibai, The Girls in Green, Spooky Stories* and *An Invitation to Die. More Spooky Stories* is her 16th book.

Three of her books, *Boots Belts Berets, A Closetful of Skeletons*, and *The Girls in Green*, are being adapted into web series.

Ajoy is a retired Army officer who has travelled all over India and has been posted to offbeat places around the country. A qualified mountaineer, he has undertaken several mountaineering and bicycle, as well as trekking expeditions in the mountains and valleys all across the Himalayas. He is fond of reading, writing, and photography.

He has co-authored three books with Tanushree. *Decoding the Feronia Files*, written by the duo, is the first Indian Cli-Fi thriller.

About the Illustrator

Sucharita Sengupta Suri is an illustrator and a graphic designer based in Mumbai, India.

She has been running her design studio for the past almost two decades. During the 2020 lockdown, she started following her passion for illustration. Currently, she pursues both graphic design and illustration projects professionally.

Sucharita is known for her art style which she calls 'whimsical paintings'. Her paintings explore the beauty and the magic in nature, fables, and fairytales.

A writer's journey turns into a nightmare when he disembarks from the train to catch a thief and misses the train.

Anirudh is forced to spend the night in a tiny railway station with barely anyone in sight. A power failure adds to his woes. Guided by the flashlight on his phone, he finds his way to the waiting room. There, he finds thirteen chairs and a dozen passengers seated in the room. The next train is due at dawn, so they decide to pass time by swapping ghost stories...

Uncover the mysteries of an ancient Egyptian tomb, travel to the ruins of an old fort and meet the ghosts of China's Forbidden City in this unusual set of eerie, spine-tingling SPOOKY STORIES!